THE TRUTH CHRONICLES

Book 4: The Thief

Tim Chaffey & Joe Westbrook

Illustrated by
Melissa "Inkhana" Mathis

Risen Books
Richmond, Kentucky

2019

The Truth Chronicles: The Thief
Copyright © 2012 by Tim Chaffey & Joe Westbrook.
All rights reserved.
Second Printing, 2019

Edited by Reagen Reed
Illustrated by Melissa "Inkhana" Mathis

www.RisenBooks.com
Risen Books is an imprint of Risen Ministries, LLC
Richmond, Kentucky

Scripture quotations are taken from the New King James Version®. Copyright © 1982 by Thomas Nelson. Used by permission. All rights reserved.

This novel is a work of fiction. Characters, plot, and incidents are products of the authors' imaginations. Characters are fictional, and any similarity to people living or dead is purely coincidental unless used with the individual's permission.

ISBN-13: 978-1-936835-08-9
E-book ISBN: 978-1-936835-09-6

Printed in the United States of America

*For all the young people or young at heart
who desire to know the truth.*

Prologue

"Man, it's hot." Rich Perkins dabbed his brow with his already moist bandana. "Do you ever get used to this?"

Bodie Vaughn swerved to miss a pothole, then glanced at the Land Rover's digital thermometer. "I don't think so." He grinned at Rich. "Why? You regretting your decision to spend your sabbatical here? It's not much hotter than that summer we spent in New Mexico back in seminary—look, only 113 degrees." Shrugging his thin shoulders, he heaved a mocking sigh. "But I bet your youth group kids would be glad to have you back early if you decide to wuss out on me."

Rich glanced at the vehicle's digital thermometer and shook his head. "I think you mean 114." He smiled, turning to stare out the windshield at the harsh Middle Eastern landscape. "I'd be lying if I said I wasn't a little homesick." He paused, then swiveled in his seat to look at the four nondescript suitcases jostling against each other in the back. "But I wouldn't miss this for anything. I love watching how people react when they get their hands on a Bible for the first time. They are so hungry for God's Word here."

"Yeah, that was really an incredible response at our last stop," Bodie said. "I've been at this for a while now, but it never gets old."

Rich nodded. After they graduated from seminary together, Bodie had taken a job with an international organization that translated and distributed Bibles in countries where it wasn't readily available. Eight months ago he had invited Rich to spend his six-month sabbatical passing out Bibles and encouraging small, secret congregations of Christians.

"It's amazing what the truth will do. Too many people take it for granted back home."

"That's for sure. With the Bible so readily accessible there, you'd think more people would listen to what it has to say."

"I just wish every pastor and church leader would spend a week over here. I mean, these people risk their lives just to own a copy of the Bible, but back home there are pastors that aren't even willing to preach from it." Rich shook his head in frustration. "I just don't get it."

"I guess that's the price you pay for being comfortable." Bodie glanced at him. "If it makes you feel any better, I'm glad you're here."

Rich was about to respond when the front tires hit a patch of loose sand on the otherwise packed dirt road, sending their SUV off to the right. Bodie overcorrected, and the back end fish-tailed. Easing off the accelerator, he straightened the vehicle out, but not before a cloud of dust sneaked through every cracked seal and ill-fitted window to coat the seats—and the men—with a fine layer of powder.

Rich coughed and reached for a bottle of water from the floor by his feet. "I don't know if I could ever get used to all of this sand." He took a drink and swished the water around in his mouth. "Guess it was a waste to shower this morning."

Bodie laughed. Then, abruptly, he leaned forward, squinting into the distance.

"What do we have here?" he asked, his laughter gone. "It looks like a checkpoint, but there isn't supposed to be one here."

Rich scanned their map. "No there isn't. And no one mentioned it before we left. It must be new."

"It's okay. Just stay calm and start praying."

As they neared the checkpoint, a man carrying a machine gun waved at them to stop. Bodie pulled over to where the man pointed and cut the ignition.

Rich focused on remaining calm, although his palms were already moist with sweat. He willed himself not to look at the suitcases in the back, each with a false bottom concealing several Bibles. The government in this area was particularly hostile toward Christians, and he knew he and Bodie could be executed for spreading the gospel. Thoughts of his wife, May, flickered through his mind, and he tried not to think about whether he would ever see her again.

The man with the machine gun walked over

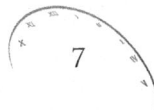

and was joined by another guard who had a pistol holstered on his belt. The insignia on his uniform designated him as a captain. Bodie rolled down the window as he approached.

The captain spoke a few quick words in Arabic, but Rich couldn't make them out.

Bodie replied calmly, also in Arabic. "*Lughati al arabic laisat kama yajib. Hal tatakallamu alloghah alenjleziah.*"

Rich recognized a few of the words and realized his friend had asked if the guard could speak English.

"Papers," the captain said in heavily accented English, his gaze never leaving Bodie's face. Rich pulled his passport from his breast pocket and handed it to Bodie, who had already drawn his identification. Upon receiving the documents, the soldier scrutinized them for several long moments before handing them back. "Out. Open back."

Fighting to keep the panic from his face, Rich stepped out of the SUV and walked to the rear. *Father, I know that You are in control of this situation. I ask that You would send Your protection for us now.*

Bodie opened the hatch and stepped aside. Rich silently prayed as the captain opened each of the suitcases and rifled through them. He watched as the man's hand brushed over the latch that released the false bottom on one suitcase. The captain paused, fingering the catch, trying to flip it to the side. When nothing happened, he moved on to the next case, and Rich exhaled quietly, shouting praises and thanks in his head.

After several more anxious moments, the man stepped back and closed the hatch, apparently satisfied. He scowled at Bodie. "In. Go."

The Americans returned to the vehicle, started it up, and drove away. It was several minutes before either could say anything.

Finally, Rich let out a deep breath. "I don't know how many more of those stops I can take. Did you see how the latch jammed when he tried to open it? I've heard missionaries talk about things like this, but it's completely different when my own life is on the line."

Bodie looked at his friend. "Maybe it didn't jam."

"What? You think he was a believer and that he just let us go?"

"Maybe. Or maybe they'll keep an eye on us to see where we take the suitcases. I don't know, so we'd better be careful. But I do know that God is watching over us, my friend. We must never forget that."

ONE

Jax Thompson grabbed the back of the seat in front of him. "We're finally here. I can't wait to get off this bus."

Izzy, Jax's best friend, nudged his right shoulder and pointed to their teacher, who had just stood up in the front of the vehicle. "We aren't getting off yet."

"Lis—" Mr. Doniger, a tall man with strawberry-blonde hair, a pointed nose, and large ears, lost his balance as the bus came to a complete stop. He reached for the pole near the driver to steady himself. Blushing, he regained his composure as several students laughed. "As I was going to say, listen up.

"Let's go over a few ground rules. Since this is a school-sponsored field trip, all of our normal rules are in place. Remember, this is a state park, so no littering. As they say, 'Leave only footprints. Take only memories.'

"Ladies, you will be staying in this cabin right in front of the bus. Guys, your cabin is a little ways down the trail to my left." He glanced at his watch. "Let's meet back here in fifteen minutes. You have a checklist of the supplies you need to bring."

Jax pulled himself up and turned to his friends JT and Micky as his fellow classmates slowly exited the bus. "This is going to be sweet. I can't wait to see these trees again."

JT stood and slung her backpack over her shoulder. "Aren't you glad you signed up for botany?"

Before he could respond, Micky said, "Maybe you can stop whining about studying plants now. That's all we've heard from you for the whole year."

Jax smiled and shook his head. "Nah, I'll start bellyaching again when spring break ends and we're back in school."

A slap on his shoulder caused Jax to turn around. Ted sported a toothy grin and William stood by his side. "Dude, I thought you said you've never been here before."

"That's right. I haven't been here."

"Then why did you say that you couldn't wait to see these redwoods again?"

Jax quickly realized that he may have said too much. He had seen redwood trees before, but that was during one of their journeys to the pre-Flood world in the time machine. He and JT had been chased through a forest by an allosaurus. He shot JT an "oops" glance and then faced Ted again. "Yeah, I've seen them before, but just not here."

Ted laughed. "Oh, well, next time be a little clearer when I'm eavesdropping."

JT stepped into the aisle and whispered. "Hopefully, Al won't be stalking us this time."

A smile crossed Jax's face, and he waited for the girls to step in front of him before following them off the bus. He moved away from the vehicle, looked up at the towering green and brown peaks surrounding him, and inhaled deeply. A robust pine scent struck his nostrils, immediately bringing a flood of memories. Ten months had passed since he and his friends had traveled to a time before Noah's Ark, but the strong aromas made it seem as if they had just been there.

"See ya in a few minutes," JT said. She and Micky turned left and headed for their cabin.

Startled from his mini-daydream, Jax started moving again. "If you're lucky."

Micky shook her head. "Dream on, Thompson."

Picking up his pace, he pulled alongside Izzy. "I'm stoked, man. This trip is going to be great." He motioned toward a giant tree to his right. "Look at this thing."

Izzy was already gazing at the enormous trunk near the edge of the trail. "You weren't kidding. These things are incredible. The diameter of this one must be at least fifteen feet."

"Amazing." Jax looked up the trail and noticed the rest of the guys were nearing the cabin. "Hey, let's hurry up and drop our stuff off."

The boys hustled over to their building and stopped to read the information sign near the front door. *This cabin was built in 2017. All of the wood for every building and piece of furniture in this campground came from a 1,700 year old tree that fell during a storm. Please treat this facility with the utmost respect.*

Jax scanned the large structure in front of him and whistled. "Can you believe this whole building was made from one tree?"

"Yeah, and it wasn't even one of the biggest. This place is still in pretty good shape too. Let's check it out."

Jax followed his friend past the front door and scanned the large common room with a kitchenette on the far left end. A group of boys sat on wooden benches surrounding an enormous coffee table whose top was fashioned from one slab of the giant tree. They seemed to be counting the number of rings.

The door to the restroom was open in front of him, and, ducking his head in, Jax could see a couple of shower stalls separated by wooden partitions. He followed Izzy into the sleeping area on the right and headed for one of the open bunk beds. "I get the top mattress."

"I don't think so."

Jax held out a fist. "Rock, paper, scissors."

Izzy nodded and prepared for the duel.

The boys pumped their fists, and Jax's scissors beat Izzy's paper.

"Ha!" Jax tossed his sleeping bag and suitcase

on the top bunk. "Come on, let's go meet up with the girls."

Izzy grabbed Jax's shirt. "Hold on a minute. Aren't you forgetting something?" He pulled out the supply list from Mr. Doniger.

"Oh, yeah. What do we need to bring?" Jax slid his backpack off his shoulder.

"Your phone for one thing," Izzy said. "We need to document the various plants we find by taking pictures of them."

The boys quickly sorted through their bags, transferring the necessary and some extra supplies into their respective backpacks: bottled water, a notebook, a field guidebook, and some trail mix Jax's mom had given to them before they left early that morning. Before long they headed to the parking lot where other students and chaperones were gathering.

While they waited for the stragglers, Jax craned his head back and stared at the treetops high above and the snippets of blue sky beyond. Moments later Izzy elbowed him and pointed toward Mr. Doniger, who was setting off down one of the main trails. After a few minutes of hiking, the group stopped near a huge rounded object that sat behind what appeared to be a small crater in the ground.

The teacher stepped forward and faced the class. "Does anyone know what this thing is behind me?"

A couple of hands went up. When called upon, a girl named Teresa asked, "Is it the bottom of one of the trees that fell over?"

Mr. Doniger nodded. "That's exactly what it is. It may be hard to believe, but the roots on a tree this size only go down ten to twelve feet and spread outward about sixty feet. The trees are virtually impervious to bugs and disease, and they can even survive forest fires. In fact, the greatest threat to a redwood is the wind."

Jax took notes as his teacher continued to provide detail after detail about the majestic trees. Ten minutes passed before they started down the path, but it wasn't long before they stopped again, this time near a fallen tree that had once blocked the path. A four-foot-wide right-of-way had been cut out of the tree to allow people to pass through.

Positioning himself in between the two halves of the fallen giant, Mr. Doniger touched the section on his right side and told the students to notice the tree rings. He explained that the appearance of the rings was due to the size of the cells produced during wetter and drier seasons. "Here we have a great example of dendrochronology or, as the average person calls it, tree-ring dating. The park service has marked off every fifty rings so that you can quickly see how old this one was. Remember, each ring represents a year. Based on the number of rings, we can say that this tree was around 640 years old when it was knocked over. So it had already been standing here for a while when Columbus set sail for America.

"These are some of the oldest living organisms in the world. A few are estimated to be about 4,000 years old. Come on up and take a look at these cross sections."

Jax moved closer to JT and Micky. He whispered, "Interesting that none of them are more than 4,300 years old, isn't it?" When confusion registered on Micky's face, he said, "You know, because they didn't survive the Flood."

"Oh, that's right," Micky said.

As if on cue, one of the boys in the group raised his hand. "Mr. Doniger? You said that these are some of the oldest living things on earth. What's older?"

"That's a good question, Dylan. Some of the bristlecone pines found in certain areas in the western United States are dated between 4,500 to 5,000 years old."

Micky looked at Jax and raised her eyebrows.

"Don't worry." He motioned toward Izzy. "He's been researching this."

"Mr. Doniger," Izzy said, "how reliable is dendrochronology?"

"It's quite reliable, Isaiah. Like I said before, trees usually produce one ring per year, so it's pretty straightforward."

"You said 'usually.' So is it possible for outside elements disrupt the growth pattern so that a tree produces two rings in a year, or maybe none at all? You know, things like bugs, frost, fire, or seismic activity."

Mr. Doniger cocked his head. "Yeah, it's true that those things can impact the growth of rings, especially if the tree's in a climate where there isn't much variation. But you can still get a decent ballpark figure by counting the rings."

Izzy quickly jotted something in his notebook. "Do you think it's possible the dates of the bristlecone pines are inflated a bit? From what I've read, it's quite difficult to even see the rings on those trees unless you use a microscope. Plus, they don't really find 4,500 rings in a row. I mean, they get samples from different growths on the trees and then try to correlate, or compare the sections and add the numbers, right?"

"Yes, that's true in many cases."

Izzy adjusted his glasses. "Also, I read that the Caribbean pines can grow as many as five rings per year. So if the climate was fairly steady when the bristlecone pines first started growing, is it possible that they put on a few rings per year? And, if that's the case, do you think that we could drop that age estimate by several hundred years?"

Jax tapped Micky with his elbow. "Told ya."

"You've really done your homework, Isaiah. I'm

impressed," Mr. Doniger said. "Sure, I think it's plausible that the ages are a bit inflated. Just like it's possible rings skipped a year once in a while. So even though it isn't an exact science, dendrochronology can give you a fairly reliable estimate of the tree's age. With the bristlecone pines, if your scenario turned out to be right, then those trees would be a bit younger, but the oldest ones are still probably more than 4,000 years old."

"Thank you, sir."

William walked past Izzy on his way to the large opening cut through the downed tree and nudged him. "Teacher's pet."

For the next few minutes, the students looked at the toppled behemoth. Some took pictures of each other in various poses up against the wood, while others milled about, chatting in their respective groups.

"Hey, everyone," Mr. Doniger said. "It's almost eleven now. I'm going to give you until twelve o'clock to work on your homework assignment. You should all have your handouts with the various plant specimens. Your job is to locate each of the plants and take pictures of them. You also have a map of this area in your packet. Mark down on the map where you found each item. Just be sure not to disturb them.

"Are there any questions?" Mr. Doniger paused. "Okay, do not wander off alone, and stay near this trail. It loops around about a mile and will take you right back to the parking lot. We'll have our lunch at 12:15, and then you'll need to get ready for the rafting trip."

About thirty minutes after Mr. Doniger set them free to gather their photo specimens, Micky glanced around the little hollow where she and JT were examining the leaves of a lacy fern. The late morning sun filtered through the forest, and patches of sunlight danced on the larger ferns alongside the trail. None of their classmates were in sight. Satisfied that they were alone, she said, "Okay, I've been reading some papers by Bornauld's group in Colorado. Based on what they've said, I think we should invert the gamma matrix."

JT looked up from the plant, biting her lower lip. "But that would really increase the power output. We would probably need to add some capacitors to the board."

Micky nodded. "And we would need another power regulator. I already checked on it, and Jeebs Electronics has one in stock that would easily handle what we need."

Concern spread across JT's face. "Are you sure about this? It could fry our whole project."

"Well, not absolutely, of course, but Bornauld's theories are convincing, and the math looks right.

I think it's a possibility. If we have time, we could write a simulation program to see if MAT could handle it."

JT rocked back on her heels and stared into space, thinking. Finally she nodded. "That could be just the thing." She grinned at Micky. "Think you can handle winning two years in a row? You know, a tele—"

"Who's Matt?" Dylan asked as he walked out from behind a nearby tree. His heavy-rimmed glasses slipped down his nose, and he shoved them back up with his finger and thumb.

Micky glared at him as Carter also stepped into view. *Man, they might be the two biggest geeks in our entire school.*

"Yeah, and what's all this about a gamma matrix?" Carter asked.

"It's none of your business," Micky said. "And even if it was, I doubt you could comprehend it."

"Micky, be nice," JT said.

"I wouldn't be so sure." Dylan put his hands on his hips. "You got lucky last year. I think your whole project was a sham, and you just tricked the judges before Ted and William allegedly disintegrated it."

Micky felt her face redden, and she clenched her fists. "What place did you guys take last year, Dylan?" She pretended to think. "Oh, that's right. Your project didn't even work."

JT put her hand on Micky's arm. "It's not worth it. Let's just go find Jax and Izzy."

Dylan smiled. "Yeah, run along to your little boyfriends. But you'd better watch that temper, Micky. It's going to get you into trouble someday."

"If you weren't such a wimp, I'd pound you, but that wouldn't be much of an accomplishment." Micky said, yanking her arm away from JT. For a moment rage threatened to overwhelm her, then she glanced at her friend's face. Something about JT's demeanor calmed her. She shrugged. "I'll just settle for whipping you guys in the fair again this year." She stomped past the guys. "Come on, girl."

Carter snickered. "We'll see about that. You girls don't have a chance of beating us."

Two

Jax whooped as water sprayed over the side of the raft and into his face. "This is great!"

Izzy held his paddle with both hands and jabbed the blade into the river, trying to steady the large raft. After pulling the paddle out of the water, he turned to Mr. Reyes. "Are you sure that was only a class two?"

Mr. Reyes laughed. "I'm positive. We'll go through a couple of class-three rapids next, and you'll definitely be able to tell the difference."

As the torrent calmed, JT looked ahead at the other rafts. Each craft carried six students and a guide, and everyone seemed to be having a wonderful time. She set her paddle on her lap and stared at the green water of the Eel River as the sunlight glistened on the ripples. *God, thank You for such a beautiful place and for this incredible trip.* She closed her eyes and instantly noticed each movement of the boat as it rocked up and down. Concentrating on the sounds, she listened to the chatter and laughter of her classmates and then inhaled deeply, letting the various scents sink in.

"Hey, JT!" Micky said.

"Yeah?"

"Wake up, girl! Are you ready for this next run?"

JT looked downstream and watched the rafts

in front of them drop below the waterline as they descended the next set of rapids. "Bring it on!"

"Okay, guys, listen up," Mr. Reyes said with his thick Spanish accent. "Ted. William. Are you guys listening?"

Ted and William stopped sword fighting with their paddles. "Sorry, dude—I mean Mr. Reyes," Ted said.

Mr. Reyes shook his head. "Pay attention. This part is going to be a little crazier than the others. You'll still need to paddle, but keep your weight shifted toward the middle of the raft. Just keep your heads in the game and listen for my instructions."

"Everybody hang on," Jax said. "Here we go."

The raft rocked front to back and side to side as it shot through the rapids. JT and her friends paddled hard while Mr. Reyes steered and called directions from the back. Twice it looked like they were going to run straight into one of the rocks sticking up out of the water, but at the last moment they veered to one side or the other. By the end of the run, each student was laughing or whooping it up as they let the current carry them toward the next set of rapids.

"That was amazing!" Jax said. "I can't wait for the next one."

"Mr. Reyes, you're really good at this," Micky said.

"Thanks. It's a lot of fun, and you guys are doing a great job."

"Have you ever flipped a raft?" Izzy asked.

"One time I did, but it was on one of my first trips, and the water was a lot higher. We really shouldn't have been out that day. But today is a great day for it, so we should be alright."

Jax turned his face so Mr. Reyes couldn't see it. "Famous last words," he said to the group.

"How long before the next run?" William asked.

"We've got a couple of minutes before it gets a little rough. Go ahead and relax a bit."

JT thought the following half-hour was some of the most fun she'd ever had, though it was also exhausting. There were several rapids close together that required a lot of paddling to get through. Her shoulders ached from the effort, but she couldn't stop smiling.

After a long series of class-two rapids, they came to a stretch where the river was wider and slower. "So is this the calm before the storm?" Izzy asked.

"Yes it is," Mr. Reyes said. "It will be calm for the next five minutes or so. After that, we'll have the toughest run of the day, and then we're done."

JT was glad for the break. She rested her paddle on her knees, leaning forward to stretch her back. After catching her breath, she massaged her shoulders and triceps and saw her friends doing the same.

"You okay, JT?" Jax asked.

"Yeah, I'm just a bit winded. How about you?"

"I'm fine. It's quite a workout, but well worth it." Jax nudged Izzy with his elbow. "How about it, Iz? Having fun yet?"

"Are you kidding? This is the best field trip ever."

"I know, right?" Micky said.

JT glanced at Ted and William, who had resumed their mock paddle fight, and she was sure they weren't listening. Mr. Reyes appeared to be studying the river ahead. "Well, it's certainly the best school-sponsored field trip."

Micky leaned in and spoke quietly. "That's true. This doesn't compare with our other adventures. Speaking of which ... Jax, is your dad ever going to let us use the car again?"

Jax matched her volume. "I told you that we couldn't use it again until we finished our project."

JT knew it was dangerous to use the time machine again. Each of their trips brought some sort of unexpected danger, plus they all had serious concerns about messing up the present by changing the past. But the thrill of being in the past and exploring an exotic world that confirmed the biblical accounts in Genesis overrode those concerns. She crossed her arms. "I don't get it. What does your latest project have to do with using the car?"

Jax grinned, and JT instantly knew she wasn't going to get the answer she wanted to hear. "I guess you'd better get used to disappointment, because we aren't talking. Right, Iz?"

"That's right," Izzy said. "You'll find out soon enough."

Micky huffed. "So after you guys finish up, we can use the car again?"

"That's what my dad told us," Jax said.

Screams erupted from ahead of them and the teens jolted. JT looked up just in time to see the back end of one of the rafts disappear from view as it descended the upcoming rapids.

"Everybody get ready. We'll be there in less than a minute," Mr. Reyes said. "This is the big one. Brace yourselves, be ready to paddle, and hang on tight."

The roar of the water increased, and Jax seemed to bristle with anticipation. JT smiled as she thought about the joy he had shown since trusting in Christ. He had been transformed. No more moody Jax full of angst. Now he loved the Lord and wasn't afraid to show it. Her smile grew even wider.

Jax saw her staring at him and returned her smile.

Blushing, JT turned away and readied herself for the next run.

"Here it comes," Mr. Reyes said. "Ready ... Go!"

JT shoved her blade into the water and pulled it through with all her might. Micky screamed as the front of the raft tipped downward. They raced through the churning water. Several rocks jutted out at odd angles. They sped toward a pair of boulders that were too close together for the raft to fit through.

Mr. Reyes fought furiously to avoid the inevitable impact. "Hold on!"

JT pulled her paddle in just as the raft slammed into one of the rocks. The impact tossed her forward and she nearly hit Izzy. The raft tipped first one way, and then the other as it hit the rocks and was lifted up. Suddenly, and without warning, the back end of the boat spun around, pulled by the overpowering current.

Relief washed over JT as she thought they were free from the maelstrom. But it quickly disappeared when the raft shuddered under another impact.

Blinded by the spray, JT closed her eyes and held on. Above the deafening blast of the water she heard Micky scream Izzy's name. She opened her eyes and looked in Izzy's direction. He wasn't there.

"Izzy!" Jax yelled.

Terror raced through JT's body as she realized her friend had gone overboard into the treacherous river. Then she heard Ted yelling for William. She spun around and quickly realized William wasn't in the boat either. "Mr. Reyes! Do something!"

"I'm trying!" Mr. Reyes placed the blade of his paddle against the rock they were stuck on and shoved hard. The raft pushed away slightly and was soon caught in the current again, rushing downstream toward the next section of churning whitewater.

JT frantically scanned the water. After a few seconds, she spotted Izzy and William being dragged along by the torrent. "I see them! Oh no!" She watched helplessly as Izzy reached out and grabbed the back of William's life preserver, just before they both slammed into a boulder.

Mr. Reyes shouted, "Keep paddling. We're almost through this. Jax, you can't help them right now!"

Her heart pounding, JT shoved her paddle into the river again and glanced at Jax, suddenly fearful that he was going to throw himself overboard in an effort to save their friends. His face was a grim mask of helpless worry, but he jammed his feet more snugly under the raft's thwart and dug his paddle into the water. When she looked back toward Izzy and William, they had vanished behind a line of jagged boulders.

She turned around and focused on doing her part, forcing herself not to imagine what might be happening to the two boys. She tried to pray, but between the demands of paddling and the tendrils of fear that kept creeping into her mind, all she could manage was a broken, *Father, please...please.*

When they rounded a bend and the current slowed a little, Jax asked, "JT, did you see them?"

She wiped her face and then nodded. "For just a moment. Izzy had a hold of William near the shore, but they crashed into a rock. I didn't see what happened after that."

"What side were they on?" Mr. Reyes asked, his eyes on the river behind them.

"The left."

"Then let's get to that shore."

They paddled silently toward the left bank. JT prayed, and, from the look on his face, so did Jax. She glanced at Micky and saw that there were tears in her eyes.

When they neared the shore, Mr. Reyes jumped out of the raft and pulled it onto dry land. He whipped out a walkie-talkie and told one of his fellow chaperones about their predicament. Returning the device to his pocket with one hand, he pulled a first aid kit out of a box lashed securely to one of the thwarts. "JT, you and Micky stay here with the raft. Make sure it doesn't get pulled into the water, and keep an eye out for the boys, just in case they didn't make it to the shore." He handed her an emergency whistle. "If you see anything, blow three short blasts on this, then wait a minute and repeat the signal. Jax, you and Ted come with me."

Jax ducked to avoid a small tree branch as he crashed through the underbrush after Mr. Reyes. The teacher didn't look back; he seemed to be muttering to himself, and there was a tense set to his shoulders.

"Are you okay, Mr. Reyes?" He saw a muscle in Mr. Reyes's jaw clench.

"That depends. You guys are my responsibility. If anything bad happens, it's my fault."

Jax shook his head, feeling sick. He couldn't bear to think about Izzy being hurt, but what had happened wasn't Mr. Reyes's fault. "You couldn't control the river."

"I know." Mr. Reyes paused and glanced back. "But that doesn't change anything."

They hiked in silence for a short time before finding a small clearing next to the river. "There they are," Ted said and then ran ahead.

"Gracias a Dios," Mr. Reyes said quietly.

Jax freed himself from a thorny plant that had latched onto his shirt and looked up. William sat against a rock, his face twisted in pain as he held his right arm against his body. Izzy, sitting on one of the nearby boulders, was no longer wearing a shirt, but had it balled up and pressed against his head.

Relief and joy swept over Jax. He wanted to jump up and down and shout thanks to God, but instead he just called out, "Are you alright?"

"I'm okay, but I got a quite a gash on my forehead." Izzy pulled his damp and reddened shirt away to reveal the cut.

Jax flinched at the sight of so much blood.

Mr. Reyes opened up the first aid kit. "I think you might need stitches. Let's get some gauze and a bandage on there to see if it helps. At least we can keep it clean until we get out of here." He spread some antibiotic cream on the dressing and pressed it against Izzy's wound. "This might sting a little. Just hold it on there nice and tight while I get some tape to hold it in place."

Scrunching his eyes up, Izzy hissed in a breath through his teeth. "Ouch. You weren't kidding."

Mr. Reyes yanked a couple of strips of tape from the roll and crisscrossed them over the gauze. "There you go. We'll get you to a local clinic to see if you'll need any stitches. Do you have any other injuries?"

"Not that I know of, but I think William broke his arm."

Mr. Reyes turned to William. "How bad is it?"

"It hurts to move," William said.

The teacher pulled an elastic bandage from the kit. "Let's get it wrapped up for now. We'll take you guys to a doctor when we get back to camp. Do you have any other injuries?"

William grunted. "I think that's it."

Mr. Reyes quickly wrapped William's arm to

immobilize it and then helped him to his feet. "Let's get back to the raft." He looked at Izzy. "Do you need any help?"

Izzy stood and took a few measured steps. "No, I'm good."

As the group hiked through the brush, Ted asked, "Mr. Reyes, what happened back there? You said this was a calm day on the river."

Mr. Reyes held back a branch as the teens passed by him. "That's one of the dangers of rafting. The water was pretty calm, and the other rafts made it through just fine." He let go of the branch. "But some of these rapids can be disastrous if you go off course just a little. We were supposed to go around the rocks to the left, but we were carried straight into them."

Jax looked at the rapids to his right and thought about the incredible force of the water. Then he recalled that JT's dad had told him how some Christians who believed in billions of years say that the Flood was worldwide, but was a tranquil flood and left no evidence. He shook his head. *They obviously don't understand how powerful water is.*

As they exited the brush, the girls ran to meet them.

"Oh, my goodness. Are you okay?" Micky asked, rushing over to Izzy, who looked far worse than he was because he had put his blood-soaked shirt back on.

Pointing to his forehead, Izzy said, "I might just need a few stitches."

She turned to William. "What'd you do to your arm?"

"I think it's broken."

Ted laughed. "Dude, you would do anything to get out of paddling."

Three

JT watched as each of the girls around the table took turns revealing the number on her card. *Six of clubs...queen of diamonds...a ten...come on! Somebody has to have something lower than my three.* Bethany, the blonde sitting to her right, grimaced as she flipped her card over. *A four.* JT held her hands out. "Seriously? I can't believe I'm already out. Three straight hands." She let her losing card drop to the enormous table made from a redwood cross-section.

The twelve girls erupted in laughter, then belted out the tune they sang every time someone was eliminated from the game.

Mara, the girl sitting directly across from JT, gathered the cards for the next deal. "That's what you get for beating me in the final round last game."

"At least you'll have a chance this game." JT smiled, then stood up and stretched. "I'm going to bed. I'll see you guys in the morning." She turned to the two chaperones sitting on a couch, grading papers. "Good night, Ms. Graham. Good night, Dr. Lynch."

"Good night, JT," Dr. Lynch said.

Several girls also wished her a good night and then turned back to their game. JT padded across the cabin floor, past the bathrooms, and then to her bunk. She grabbed her Bible from her backpack and climbed up to the top mattress, a task made much more difficult by tired arms and sore shoulders from the day's rafting trip. She fluffed her pillow and then slid into her sleeping bag.

Taking a deep breath, she closed her eyes and let the events of the day flash through her memory. *Dear God, thank You for keeping Izzy and William safe today—well, relatively safe. Please help William's arm and Izzy's cut get better soon. Thanks for an amazing trip so far. Help me to honor You with my life, and please teach me from Your Word as I read. Amen.*

Opening to her bookmarked page, she pulled out her light and clipped it to the top of the book. As she immersed herself in reading a few chapters of Daniel, she soon forgot the laughing and singing in the next room, gripped by the account of Daniel in the lion's den. Upon finishing the chapter, she prayed, *God, please help me to be as bold as Daniel, so that I will follow You at all times, even if my life is threatened.*

"Hey, JT, you still awake?" Mara asked.

JT turned and saw the slender brunette standing by the bed. "Oh, I didn't even know you were there. So you didn't fare any better without me?"

Mara chuckled. "No, not really. I think I was the fourth one out. So whatcha reading?"

JT held it up so her friend could see the front cover. "It's my Bible."

"Really? I didn't know anybody really read that unless they were a preacher or something."

"Actually, I try to read through mine every year."

Confusion registered on Mara's face. "Why?"

JT rolled to her side and propped herself up on an elbow. "Because it's God's Word, and I want to know it as well as possible."

"God's Word? You think God actually wrote it?"

"No, He didn't write it, but the Bible says that the people who did write it were inspired, or guided by God."

"So what about all of the myths that are in there?" Mara asked. "Did He inspire them to write things that aren't true?"

JT thought Mara sounded sincere in her questions, even though she had challenged her beliefs. She paused before answering the question, and then remembered some advice her dad had told her. *When someone says there are contradictions or errors in the Bible, just hand it to them and ask them to show you where they are.*

She held out her Bible. "Here, can you show me what you're talking about? What myths?"

Mara looked at the book but didn't grab it. "It's not like I'd know where they are, but doesn't the Bible have stories about a talking snake, unicorns, zombies, and giants? Do you really believe that stuff?"

JT giggled. "Zombies? Where did you hear that?"

"My brother. I heard him ripping on Christians before, and he said that you guys believe in a zombie sky god. Is that true?"

"No, that's not even close to what the Bible teaches. God isn't just a sky god. He's God over all things. He made everything and cares for it. He's the only true God."

Mara stood on the first step of the ladder near the head of the bunk bed. "So where does the zombie thing come in?"

"I'm not sure. Maybe it's from people trying to mock Christians. Christianity is based on Jesus, the Son of God, dying on a cross and then rising from the dead three days later."

"Sounds like a zombie to me."

JT shook her head. *Duh, I forgot to clear that up.* "Sorry, I guess if I say it like that, it kind of does. Only Jesus walked and talked with people, and He still taught them, so He wasn't a mindless undead body." JT flipped to Luke 24, and showed Mara verses 36–42. "And He wasn't some sort of ghoul or ghost, either. Take a look here. He had a physical body and told His followers they could touch Him to see that He wasn't a ghost. He even ate with them."

Mara laughed. "If He was a zombie, He would have eaten *them*." She quickly covered her mouth.

"Oh, I'm sorry. I hope I didn't offend you. I was just trying to be funny."

"No problem. I didn't think you were trying to be offensive."

"Okay, but what about the talking snake, the unicorn, and…and—"

"David and Goliath?" JT asked.

Mara's eyes lit up. "That's it. David and Goliath. That's definitely in the Bible, right? Do you really think David killed a giant? It sounds like a fable about never giving up or something."

"David and Goliath?" Bethany asked, approaching from the hall. "Are you guys talking about the Bible?"

JT heard the disdain in her voice, and her stomach tightened. "Yeah."

Bethany pointed at the Bible. "Why are you reading that?"

"That's what I asked her before," Mara said.

Taking a deep breath, JT tried to steady herself. It was one thing to talk about her beliefs with someone as honestly curious as Mara, and something else entirely to discuss them with someone like Bethany.

"Because it's the Word of God," she said after a pause. "And I want to be sure that I'm doing what He expects from me."

Bethany snickered. "That's a good one, JT. So do you think the earth is flat, too?"

"Knock it off, Bethany," Mara said. "I want to hear what she was going to say about David and Goliath."

"Yeah, what about David and Goliath, JT?" Bethany asked. "So a little pipsqueak allegedly kills a giant with a sling, right? You don't seriously believe that, do you?"

JT sensed her temperature rising and took a calming breath. *If they're going to reject God, make sure it isn't because of my actions.* "You're right," she said. "I don't believe that."

Bethany stopped giggling, and her mouth hung open while she stared at JT.

Mara looked disappointed. "But you just told me that you believe—"

"I do," JT said quickly. "I believe the Bible is true. Every word of it."

"Then how can you say you don't believe in David and Goliath?" Mara asked.

"I didn't say that. I said I don't believe a little pipsqueak killed a giant with a sling."

"You sound like a politician," Bethany said. "You either believe little David killed a giant like the Bible says, or you don't. So which is it?"

"What if there's a third option?" JT flipped through her Bible. "If you'd give me a few seconds, I'd be happy to explain. Okay, here it is. The account of David and Goliath is in 1 Samuel 17. It's true that Goliath is described as a giant. It's also true that David used a sling and a stone, which was actually a pretty deadly weapon. But it isn't true that David was a little pipsqueak. You may have heard that in Sunday school, but it isn't what the Bible says."

"What are you talking about? Why would everybody teach it that way if the Bible doesn't say it?" Bethany asked.

"I asked my dad the same thing." JT sat up in her bed. "He said there are probably a bunch of reasons, like maybe some of them just try to simplify it for kids. When you dig deeper, though, there are several things that show David was actually a pretty big guy.

"In the previous chapter, which may have taken place several years earlier, David is described as the youngest of his brothers, so some people get the idea that he was small. But look at what it says later in that chapter. She flipped back a page and pointed to a highlighted section. "Mara, what does this say?"

Mara turned the book around and read, "Then one of the servants answered and said, 'Look, I have seen a son of Jesse the Bethlehemite, who is skillful in playing, a mighty man of valor, a man of war, prudent in speech, and a handsome person; and the LORD is with him.'" She looked up and asked, "Is this about David?"

"Yep, and—"

"So David was quite the ladies man, huh?" Bethany said.

JT ignored the comment. "And notice that this is the chapter *before* he kills Goliath, and it calls him a 'mighty man of valor, a man of war.' But that's not all. Check this out."

JT ran her finger up the page to another highlighted verse. "Look, the beginning of this chapter describes when David was anointed as king. He was the youngest of eight boys. When Samuel, the guy who anointed him, saw David's oldest brother, he was like, 'Wow, this must be the next king,' because of his physical stature."

"So? That doesn't prove anything," Bethany said.

"Actually, it means David would have probably had similar genetics to his oldest brother," Mara said. "Is that where you were going with this?"

"Exactly," JT said. "He didn't fight Goliath immediately after this. The Bible says that David was young at this time, but it never says he was small."

"Okay, but there's no guarantee he would be as big as his brother," Bethany said.

"That's true," JT said. "But look at this." She turned to chapter 17 again. "In the chapter where David fights Goliath, there are some more clues about his size. He's already been serving as the king's armor-bearer for some time, but had gone home to help his dad with the animals. When he returned, Goliath had challenged Israel's army and everyone was afraid of him, except David. He went right to King Saul and offered to kill the giant."

"Right, and that's when Saul laughed at him because he was just a little guy," Bethany said.

"No, it never says that. It says that Saul gave David his armor for the battle."

Bethany placed her hands on her hips and clicked her tongue. "I know, JT. I was in Sunday school too. David couldn't use the armor because it didn't fit."

JT shook her head. "I know that's what we were always taught back then, but it doesn't say that either. David said that he couldn't use the armor because he had not tested it yet. He wasn't used to it." She pointed to the highlighted section she had just read from and then squinted to read her note next to the verse. "Earlier in this book, it says that King Saul was a head taller than everyone in Israel. In other words, he was one of the tallest guys in the nation. Why would the king, a tall man, offer his armor to a little guy? That doesn't make any sense. If David was a little guy, Saul could have just found a soldier who was about David's size and make him give up his armor."

For once, Bethany was silent, so JT kept going. "David told Saul that when he was a shepherd, he had killed a lion and a bear with his bare hands. Later on, it says David was able to wield Goliath's sword, which was probably very big since the rest of his weapons were large. The fact is that David was probably a very strong, big guy. He wasn't as big as Goliath, but he was probably close to the size of Saul, otherwise the king wouldn't have offered him his armor."

"That makes sense," Mara said.

"Okay, well so what?" Bethany asked. "It doesn't prove any of that ever happened."

JT paused as she heard another round of the elimination song echo from the other room, followed by some trash talk from Micky. "You're right, Bethany. The fact that David was a mighty man of valor doesn't prove that everything happened. But since the Bible says it happened, then I believe it did." JT looked at Mara, who had been hanging on every word. "But it goes to show that a lot of times when people ridicule the Bible for something, they are actually ripping on a caricature of it. If you take the time to read and study it, you'll see that it makes a lot of sense." She glanced up and noticed Micky had just joined the group around her bed.

"Alright, what have I been missing?" Micky asked.

"Not much," Bethany said, pulling her long blonde hair over her shoulder and examining the ends. "JT's just been telling us Bible stories."

"Is that true, JT?" Ms. Graham asked from

the small hallway between the two main rooms. The stocky, middle-aged teacher entered the bedroom and glared at JT. "Are you talking about Bible stories?"

"They aren't just stories, Ms. Graham," JT said. "I would call them biblical accounts."

Ms. Graham noticed the Bible on the bed and her eyes opened wide. "JT Bankers! You aren't allowed to have a Bible on this trip. Hand it over."

JT saw the grin on Bethany's face and felt her own cheeks flush. She wanted to lash out but knew it would only make things worse. Instinctively, she pulled her Bible up close. "With all due respect, Ms. Graham, I have the right to bring my Bible on this trip, just like I'm allowed to bring it to class with me anytime I want. There aren't any school rules against it."

"Are you challenging my authority, Miss Bankers?"

"No, ma'am. In fact, I was just going to say that even though I have the right, I am willing to put it back in my bag." She rubbed her thumb along the binding. "But I won't let you confiscate it."

Ms. Graham still looked upset. "JT, you aren't allowed to push your religion on the other students."

"But, Ms. Graham, she wasn't pushing her religion on anyone," Mara said. "She was reading it quietly, and I came over and asked her about it."

"Mara, I would appreciate it if you did not get involved in this," Ms. Graham said.

"Chill, Ms. Graham," Micky said. "She wasn't doing anything wrong."

"Don't you start with me."

"I'm not trying to start anything, but look where we are." Micky motioned to JT's bed. "Everyone is gathered around JT. It doesn't look like she went around trying to force her beliefs on anyone."

The chaperone looked down at her watch and huffed. "You girls need to be in bed in ten minutes." She turned around and left the room, calling back over her shoulder, "I want that book put away, Miss Bankers."

When she had gone, JT looked at Micky and let out a long breath. *If only she would be that determined to know God instead of just to win an argument.* "Thanks for defending me, Micky. And you, too, Mara." JT climbed off the bunk and put her Bible in her backpack.

Mara appeared unsure how to respond and quickly shot a glance at Bethany. "Wow, what was her problem?"

"Problem? I think she was right," Bethany said.

"How was she right?" Mara asked.

"Duh, Mara. Ever heard of the separation of church and state? This is a school trip, so we have to abide by school rules."

Mara huffed. "Oh, knock it off. You and I both know JT didn't break any rules."

JT pulled herself back up on her bed. "Besides, that whole separation of church and state idea isn't found in the Constitution, and most people get it backward. The First Amendment guarantees the freedom of religion and guarantees that the government cannot make everyone follow one official religion. Having a student bring a Bible to school is not the same as the whole school saying that everyone has to be a Christian in order to graduate."

"And we go to a private school with no rules against it," Micky said. "So that wouldn't apply even if it you were right."

Bethany looked smugly at Micky. "Since when did you get all religious? Is it from hanging out with JT?"

"Who said anything about being religious?" Micky asked. "I'm just defending my friend from a double standard. What gives you the right to push your ideas if JT isn't allowed to talk about hers?'

Bethany stepped toward Micky and stared defiantly at her. "Because my views don't include belief in an invisible God who orders His people to kill other people, and then, if you don't believe in Him, He sends you to hell."

Micky didn't back down, but she didn't say anything. Slowly, she turned to JT as if asking for help.

Just stay calm. "Bethany, if you are really interested in discussing this topic, I'd be happy to do it. But if all you want to do is mock or attack my beliefs, then we won't get anywhere. I'm not interested in fighting with you, but I would suggest you examine your own beliefs before attacking others. If you sincerely believe that we're nothing but rearranged star dust—a cosmic accident—then what's the point in arguing? What point is there to life, for that matter? If God exists, then everything matters. But if there is no God, then matter is all that exists, and nothing really matters. So there would be no point to argue this."

"You're so self-righteous, JT," Bethany said. "You act like you're little Miss Perfect, but you're no better than anyone else."

"I never said I was better than anyone else, because I'm not. I'm a sinner just like everyone else, but I've been forgiven of my sins."

"That's enough!" Ms. Graham shouted from the entryway. "Now break it up, and get ready for bed. Lights off in five minutes."

As the girls scattered, JT threw her head back on the pillow. She closed her eyes to calm herself and pray. Before she could formulate a thought, a hand rested on her shoulder.

"I'm sorry I got you into trouble with Ms. Graham," Mara said.

"That's okay. I love discussing the Bible and

would do it again if I had the chance." She smiled and then whispered, "Although I have to admit, I'm glad I don't have her as a teacher this year."

Mara giggled. "Me too. Thanks for explaining things to me. Good night." She headed toward the bathroom.

"Good night, Mara."

FOUR

"Good morning, hikers." Mr. Doniger stepped up onto a park bench to address the assembled students. "Chaperones, is everybody here?"

"No, I'm missing one," Mr. Reyes said. "Has anyone seen Carter?"

Micky glanced around. *I wish we could just leave without him.*

"He said he'll be out in a minute," Dylan said.

"There he is," another student said, pointing down the trail that led to the guys' cabin.

Mr. Doniger waited for Carter to join the group. "Okay, now that we're all here, I'm going to turn it over to Ms. Graham. She's our expert hiker."

Ms. Graham stepped forward. "Listen very carefully. First thing I want you to do is to take off your backpack and double-check, even triple-check to make sure you have everything you're supposed to bring. Last year we had a student who only brought one bottle of water. This is a fifteen-mile hike, and it is going to get hot today. So make sure you have plenty of fluids."

A couple of students groaned, but everyone complied by slipping off their packs and sorting through their items.

When the hubbub died down, Ms. Graham continued, "Just like yesterday, you are to take pictures of each plant species on your list, but do not disturb the plants themselves. Make sure that any food and snacks are sealed in plastic bags. Bears and cougars are sometimes spotted in these areas. They typically avoid people, especially large groups, but it's better to be safe than sorry. For those of you who don't think you can make it the whole way, there is a spot about five miles down the trail where it crosses the road. We'll have a vehicle there to pick you up and bring you back here to the campground.

"Remember, this isn't a race. Dr. Lynch will be in the lead, so no one is allowed to run ahead of her. I will stay back and move at a slower pace in case any of you lag behind. Mr. Doniger and Mr. Reyes will be somewhere in the middle. Stay in groups of four or more, work on your assignments, and have fun."

Jax looked at Izzy, JT, and Micky. "You guys wanna hang back and take our time today?"

Micky looked at JT then shrugged. "Sure. We're not in a hurry."

The four teens waited as their classmates headed into the woods. Micky stepped into a patch of sunlight, trying to warm herself.

"How's your head feeling today?" JT asked.

"It's okay," Izzy said. "I've got a slight headache, but it's no big deal. The worst part is the stitches. They're so itchy."

"I'm just glad it wasn't any worse," Micky said.

Izzy smiled. "Thanks. Me too."

Ms. Graham motioned for them to move along. "Let's get going." In spite of the brusque words, the smile on her face revealed that she was definitely in a much better mood than the night before.

Micky and her friends entered the forest, while Ms. Graham hung back for a few minutes, apparently unwilling to hike the whole way with their group. For the next two hours they studied their surroundings, marveling at the beauty and splendor of the scenery. During that time, they stopped on a few occasions to document various plants, including an evergreen huckleberry, a rhododendron, and a thimbleberry.

The temperature climbed steadily as the sun rose higher in the sky. Micky wiped some sweat off her forehead with the back of her hand. "Man, it's getting hot."

"I was just thinking that." JT pulled off her sweatshirt and tied it around her waist.

Jax pointed ahead to where two logs rested on the ground, flanked by a few sawn sections set on end so they could be used as stools. "That looks like a good place to rest."

When they reached the logs, the teens sat and pulled out a snack and something to drink.

Micky felt the cool water rush down her throat. *That sure hit the spot.* She closed the lid on her canteen and returned it to the side pocket of her backpack.

"I can't get that song out of my head," Izzy said.

"What song?" JT asked.

"'The Parade of the Ewoks' from *Return of the Jedi*."

Jax chuckled. "I know, I keep expecting Wicket to show up somewhere in these woods."

"The parade of the what?" JT asked. "What are you guys talking about?"

Jax sighed. "I'm so disappointed, JT. How can you not recognize a *Star Wars* reference?"

JT placed her fists on her hips. "Um, maybe because I've never seen any those movies. Besides, what does this place have to do with *Star Wars*?"

"They filmed a lot of *Return of the Jedi* in the redwoods, and Wicket was an Ewok, a little bear-like creature that lived in the trees."

"Sounds pretty cheesy, if you ask me," Micky said.

"Hey, they're only some of the best movies ever made," Izzy said. "That settles it. One of these days we're going to have a *Star Wars* marathon."

Jax cleared his throat. "Well, maybe just episodes four through six. They don't need to see the first three."

"But I thought you said there were some New Age ideas in those movies," JT said.

"There are," Jax said. "But we could do what

your family does when you guys watch movies. You know, pausing it whenever certain things come up. Besides, they're still great stories, and then you two could be almost as cool as Izzy and me."

Micky laughed. "So watching those movies will make our coolness level drop that much?"

Jax smiled. "Touché."

"Hey, check these out," Izzy said. He jumped up and ran to the other side of the trail. "I think this is a salmonberry plant."

Jax pulled out his phone and snapped several pictures, including close-ups of the red berries, while JT, Micky, and Izzy compared the plant to pictures in the field guide. "So what's the consensus?"

"It's definitely a salmonberry plant," Micky said. "That's one more down and seven more to go."

Izzy walked several steps from the path. "I wonder if we might find some other species on or around this fallen tree."

Micky followed Izzy over to the downed giant. Even lying down, the tree was several feet taller than she was, and ferns had grown up all around it. "Try not to step on any of the ferns," she called over her shoulder to Jax and JT.

Izzy reached up and ran his hand along the fluted bark. "Jax, help me up. I want to see if there's anything growing on top of this."

Jax held his hands together and allowed Izzy to

use them as a step. Izzy pulled himself up, while Jax continued to push him from below.

"You girls want a lift?" Jax asked.

JT shook her head. "No, I think I'll just stay down here and look around."

"Same with me," Micky said. "But we'll help you if you want to go up there."

"Definitely." Before long, thanks to the assistance of JT and Micky, he had joined Izzy on the top of the tree.

JT turned to Micky. "I'll go around to the right if you want to go around to the left. We can meet up on the other side."

With a nod, Micky walked beside the tree, scanning the ground. She knelt down periodically to touch a leaf or wood chip or to run her fingers through the dirt. Everything smelled clean and fresh, and it reminded her of her trips to the past with the others. *That was truly an exotic location.* She knew there wasn't anything like that anywhere in the world today. She thought about the debates and discussions she'd had with her friends. *They've been able show how everything we see lines up with the Bible, and I've even seen some of it for myself—dinosaurs and man living at the same time and the stars being in almost the same position that they are today.*

She had arrived near what was once the top of the tree, and she stepped over it and started back the other way. *I can't deny what I've seen. Plus, Jax and Izzy have changed so much in the past year since they started believing in God.* Her heart felt as if it were being torn apart. Something inside told her she should just fall to her knees and cry out to God to save her. She knew she was sinful and needed His forgiveness, but something held her back.

Micky moved her right hand to her left shoulder blade and traced the scar that ran a few inches down her back. Tears formed at the edge of her eyes, and she felt her lower lip tremble as bile rose in her throat. *No. There has to be another explanation. The Bible can't be right. If there is a God, then He can't be anything like JT says. There's too much evil in this world.* A tear ran down her cheek and dropped onto her shoe. She stared at the moist spot as her mind drifted. *But I need them to accept me. They're the only people who truly care about me.*

"How's it going down there?" Izzy asked. "Did you find anything?"

Startled by his voice, Micky quickly gathered her thoughts and wiped her eyes with the back of her hand. She looked up and saw Izzy still standing on the tree, his feet at her eye-level. "Nothing we haven't seen already. How about you?"

"Nope. Nothing. Although the view is pretty cool from up here." Izzy jumped to the ground and joined her. "Here comes JT. Let's see if she did any better."

They walked along the side of the enormous tree until they met up with JT. "So did you find anything?" Micky asked.

JT shook her head. "Just ferns. How about you guys?"

"Not a thing," Micky said. "Let's get Jax and get back to the trail."

"Hi, are you kids with those other groups I passed earlier?" a middle-aged woman asked as she approached Jax, Izzy, JT, and Micky on the trail. One long brown braid hung over her shoulder, falling nearly to her waist, and she held a flyer in her hand.

"Um, yeah," Jax said.

"Here, take one of these and find out how you can help save Mother Earth." She handed the paper to him before walking rapidly past them without another word.

Puzzled, Jax watched her pass by. *What is this?* He unfolded the flyer as his friends gathered around.

"What's it say?" Micky asked.

"Looks like some type of environmentalist literature," Izzy said.

"This part talks about how these woods were spared from logging because of the efforts of conservationists," Jax said, pointing to the first column on the page.

"Here, look at this," Izzy said. "It says, 'It is humankind's duty to protect these precious redwoods and the plants and animals that live among them from people who would seek to destroy this ecosystem because of their greed.'"

Jax laughed.

"What's so funny?" Micky asked. "Don't you think we should protect the environment?"

Turning serious, Jax said, "Of course. I wasn't laughing at the idea of taking care of the environment. I'm thrilled that people have protected this place from logging. I was laughing at the inconsistencies in the worldview of the people who printed this."

"What do you mean?" Micky asked. "What inconsistencies?"

He turned to the front page of the flyer. "Look, at the bottom it says, 'Protecting 100 million years of evolution.'"

"Okay, so this group believes in evolution," Micky said. "How is that not consistent?"

"Well, if evolution were true, then it's survival of the fittest, right?"

"Obviously that's oversimplifying it," she said.

"I agree, but the principle is the same," Jax said. "Think about it. If we evolved through chance random processes, then there is no such thing as 'humankind's duty' because there would be no ultimate standard for right and wrong."

"Exactly," Izzy said. "Besides, if humans are the pinnacle of evolution, then if anyone gets to decide what is right or wrong, it would be us, right?"

Micky bit her bottom lip. "Yeah, I suppose."

"Okay, so if we're at the top, then we can protect or destroy anything we want. So a consistent evolutionist cannot tell anyone what their duty is," Izzy said.

"But we should take care of the environment," Micky said.

Izzy pointed to himself. "I agree, but on what basis can an evolutionist make that statement?"

She stared at the ground, as if searching for an answer.

JT put her hand on Micky's shoulder. "We all believe in taking care of our surroundings. The Bible teaches that we need to be good stewards of what God has given us, and that includes the environment we live in. In fact, He placed man in charge of this world, so taking care of it is actually in harmony with a biblical worldview."

"I understand what you're saying," Micky said. "But if that's true, then how come some Christians are big polluters and some evolutionists are the biggest protectors of nature?"

"People aren't always consistent with their worldview." JT grabbed the flyer from Jax and quickly scanned the back page. "I won't deny that some Christians have been irresponsible in this area, and many others. You'll find conservationists and polluters among Christians and evolutionists. But here's one of the biggest problems." She pointed to a line on the flyer. "It says, 'Planet Earth needs your help. Please donate your time or money to help save our Mother.' You see, a lot of people treat the earth as if it were a goddess or something, and some actually worship it. The Bible talks about those who end up worshiping the creature instead of the Creator. These groups might be doing a good thing in caring for the environment, but it's become a form of idolatry for them. And the sad part is that they end up caring more about nature than they do about people, who are made in the image of God."

"Don't you think you're exaggerating a bit?" Micky asked.

"I don't think she is," Jax said. "When I was in elementary school, instead of the Pledge of Allegiance, we did a pledge to the earth, and it had the same sort of lines as that flyer. I've also seen videos of people kneeling down before trees and wailing because the trees were allegedly in so much pain. Not everyone takes it that far, but there are people who do."

"Hmm," Izzy said as he gently scratched the stitches in his forehead. "I never thought about it this way before. This flyer sort of gets it right. It blames man for the destruction of the environment. Like you said, JT, there are some people who do hurt the environment, but the weather and natural disasters do far more damage than we could ever do, barring nuclear war." He held his arms out. "But since God made a perfect world and Adam's sin is responsible for all of the bad things we see, then all the damage is still sort of man's doing."

"That's true," JT said. "But that's obviously not what the people who made this handout believe."

"No, I agree. I just found it interesting that it really is our fault. And even though the Flood was caused by God, He did it because of man's wickedness. So the biggest environmental disaster in history was man's fault."

"Speaking of disasters," Jax said, tucking the flyer into the back pocket of his jeans, "we still need to find three more plant species before this hike is over."

Izzy pushed a button on his watch. "Yeah, it's already 3:00 and we have about five more miles to hike."

JT jumped and clapped. "Let's do this."

Jax smiled. *I love how excited she gets about these discussions.* He looked at Micky, who was staring at the ground and kicking at an exposed root. "You ready, Micky?"

Micky stirred from her apparent introspection. "Um, yeah. Let's go."

FIVE

"So still no breakthroughs," Micky said as she strode into the classroom.

"Did you check to see if Jeebs still had the parts?" JT asked.

"Yep, they do. Did you want to pick 'em up after school?"

"Sure. I should be able to come over afterward too, so we can get right to work." She thought about how incredible it would be to instantly transport matter from one location to another. She leaned in close to Micky and whispered, "If our invention works, then we wouldn't ever have to go to the store to pick up parts again."

JT noticed a small crowd had gathered around William. "Ooh, let me sign it." She set her books on her desk and pulled out a black marker. "How does it feel?"

"Not too bad." He held up his cast-covered arm. "It was just a hairline fracture, so I only need to keep this on for a few weeks." He touched his side with his other hand. "I've got a couple of bruised ribs too. You wanna see?"

William began to pull his shirt up with his good arm, but Micky blocked it. "That is a sight I *do not* need to see."

"It's your loss." He winked at her. "I'm just bummed that I missed out on the hike."

JT scribbled her name and handed the marker to Micky. "Well, I'm glad it wasn't too serious."

Micky also autographed the cast. "You know, if Izzy hadn't fallen in too, I would have come up with a smart remark about your lack of intelligence."

William laughed. "I wouldn't expect anything else from you, Micky. Thanks for the signatures, ladies."

"No problem," JT said before returning to her desk. After pulling out her textbook, she saw Jax enter the room and approach Izzy's desk. He waited a few moments to be acknowledged, but Izzy kept reading. Jax hefted his own textbook and let it drop with a booming thud, making Izzy jump.

"What? Oh, Jax, it's you," Izzy said.

Jax bent down to pick up his book. "You seem pretty intent. What're you working on?"

"I'm trying to identify a fungus I found on my shoe after our trip." Izzy lifted the cover of his book to show Jax it was a reference book on mycology. "It's tough, though. I think I at least have it narrowed down to a genus."

"You're such a nerd," Jax said.

Before Izzy could respond, Mr. Li entered the room. "Good morning, students. I hope those of you who went on the botany field trip over the weekend had a good time, or at least a better time than Mr. Reyes." Mr. Li set his briefcase on the desk. "He's dealing with some poison ivy right now, so I'll be substituting this morning. And since I'm not an expert in organic chemistry, you guys can use this hour as a study hall." A few mild cheers broke out, and Mr. Li sat down. "Let me remind you that the science fair is less than a month away. I can try to help you with any problems you may be having with your project or with any physics homework."

JT leaned over toward Micky. "Let's go see if he has any ideas that could help us with that physics problem."

"Okay, just a minute." Micky continued flipping through her notes. "Let me double check this first."

JT closed her notebook and waited for Micky. Moments later, they approached the teacher's desk, where Dylan and Carter stood talking to Mr. Li, presumably about their project. "Yeah, we'll try that," Dylan said. "Thanks, Mr. Li."

Dylan spun around and nearly bumped into Micky.

"Watch where you're going," Micky said.

"Well, if it isn't the two frauds," Dylan said. He lowered his voice. "Are you gonna try to pay Mr. Li off again?"

Micky pushed him. "Get away from me."

Mr. Li must have noticed the altercation. He raised his voice to make sure Dylan could hear him. "Ah, Micky and JT. How are last year's science fair champions doing?"

JT looked back and noticed Dylan shaking his head. She faced Mr. Li. "We're doing well. How are you?"

"I'm fine. Thanks for asking."

"We really miss your class, Mr. Li. Hopefully, we'll have you next year," Micky said.

He brightened. "Well, I miss having you guys in class. Now what can I help you with?"

Micky glanced around and then showed him the page in her notebook. "Are you familiar with the Addlesburg Principle?"

He lowered his glasses and stared at the diagram for a moment. "It sounds familiar. Doesn't it have to do with—"

"Shh, not so loud," Micky said.

"Oh, I almost did it again, didn't I?"

JT smiled, glad that Mr. Li hadn't blurted out the subject of their invention like he had the year before.

"Matter teleportation?" His words could barely be heard.

"That's right. We're calling it MAT. And I think we've almost got it," Micky said.

"Really?" Mr. Li looked up, his eyes bright. "Have you had any successful tests?"

"Not exactly. But we're still waiting on a couple of parts," JT said.

"You two sure aim high. So how can I help?"

Micky set her notebook on the desk and pulled out a pencil. "We really just need some help with the quantum physics involved."

He smiled broadly. "Well, you came to the right place."

For the next ten minutes, Mr. Li walked the girls through a problem. When they reached the solution, he asked, "Does that make sense?"

JT let out a deep breath. "Yeah, it seems pretty clear now. How do you keep all those numbers and variables straight?"

"It's always come naturally to me. I guess some people just have a head for numbers. You know, Isaiah does pretty well with this stuff. He could probably help you if you get stuck."

"We know," Micky said. "But we didn't want him to know what we were working on."

"Ah, I see. Alright. Well, good luck with the project. I'm looking forward to a successful demonstration at the science fair. That might be good enough for you to be the first back-to-back winners of the science fair. Not even Jonas Ellis managed to do that."

"Thanks," Micky said and grinned. "We're looking forward to winning again."

"Thanks, Mr. Li." JT headed back to her desk and said to Micky, "That problem's out of the way. Now we just need to pick up the parts."

"Only a few more hours," Micky said.

"I know. I can hardly wait."

JT stopped when she reached her desk. *Why is my notebook open? And to that page?* She looked around the room to see if anyone looked suspicious. The other students seemed completely focused on their own work.

"I'm sure glad Mr. Li helped us through that problem," JT said as she stepped out of the passenger door. "That opened up several possibilities."

Micky pulled the bag of new equipment out of the backseat of the car. "What do you mean?"

JT walked around the vehicle and joined her. "Look." She pointed to an equation on the paper. "If this is right, then the containment problem on reassembly should be much easier than we thought before."

"Meaning?"

"Meaning the energy requirements on the receiving end would be minimal."

"How minimal?"

JT took the bag from her and handed her the paper. "Unless I'm looking at this wrong, I think a normal outlet could handle it."

"Seriously?" Micky peered at the paper, her eyes darting back and forth as she read the notes.

"Yeah."

"If that's true, then it will be a lot easier to demonstrate at the science fair, and—"

"And much easier to mass produce so that everyone could have one."

Micky raised her hands in the air and jumped. "Come on, girl. We gotta get this working."

They entered the house and a strong curry scent invaded JT's nostrils. "Mmm, is that your mom's chicken tikka masala I smell?"

"Yep. Want to stay for dinner?"

"Definitely."

Before they reached the door for the basement, Micky's mother called out, "Come in here for a minute."

They walked to the living room, where a small woman sat in a recliner watching a game show. Her frazzled short black hair was highlighted with wisps of gray on the sides.

"Hi, Mom. Can JT stay for dinner?"

Micky's mom paused the television with the remote and looked up. "Oh, hi, JT. Of course. We'd love to have you join us." She turned to her daughter. "Micky, I'm sorry, but I need the car on Saturday. I have to be in the city all day."

Micky scowled and crossed her arms. "But, Mom, I needed it for the reunion."

"Well, there's nothing I can do about it. I just found out at work. You can call your father to come pick you up."

"I have a better idea." Micky turned to JT. "How would you like to drive me to my family reunion on Saturday?"

"How far away is it?" JT asked.

"It's not too far," Ms. Simmons said. "Only about an hour."

"I need to check with my parents first and make sure I can use the car, but it sounds like fun to me."

"Cool. Mom, we've gotta get going on our project downstairs." She leaned over and kissed her mother. "We're getting really close to being done with it."

"Okay, Mick. Make me proud—just like last year."

"Bye, Ms. Simmons," JT said before heading toward the basement door.

A few minutes later, after JT had called her parents to clear her new dinner plans, she and Micky busied themselves installing some of the new parts on MAT. The rectangular device in front of them was just over a foot tall and about half that in width. Sticking out from the side of the contraption was a metal arm which housed the "demolecularizer," as they jokingly called it. Theoretically, an object would be placed under the arm, which would first scan, then transform the item into energy that could be sent to a receiving device anywhere in the world. The receiver would transform the energy back into the original matter. That was the theory, anyway. In practice, they hadn't even finished constructing either device.

"So have you figured out what the guys are making yet?" Micky asked.

"No, I thought that by now they would have slipped up and told us."

"Jax said his dad won't let us use the time machine again until they finish their project. So it obviously has something to do with that."

JT ripped the shrink wrap from a package. "So whatever it is, it must make time travel safer in some way."

"Right. Maybe they've figured out a way to add power to the repulsors we made for it."

JT thought about Micky's suggestion for a few moments. "I don't think so. That wouldn't make any sense for a project, because they wouldn't be able to enter it in the science fair without revealing the power source. I don't think they'd make that same mistake again."

"Okay, then let's dive into the realm of sci-fi. The guys love those old movies. Maybe they got some harebrained idea from one of those shows." Micky pulled off her safety goggles and set the handheld grinding tool on the counter.

"Like what? What would make time travel safer?"

"How about a sonic weapon that would just scare away predators rather than hurting them?"

"That would make it safer for the people going back in time," JT said. "But I think there's more to it than that. I think he wants to make sure that we don't disturb the past at all." She looked at the ceiling and thought about possibilities. "So what could they make that would do that?"

"Definitely not a weapon then." Micky thought for a moment, then laughed. "How about some kind of neuralyzer that would erase the memory of anyone who saw them?"

JT rolled her eyes. "That seems pretty far-fetched and dangerous. They'd pretty much have to be neurologists to do something like that."

"That's true, but it would be fun to test on people like Dylan."

JT giggled. "Okay, but seriously. How could they avoid interfering with the past?"

"I guess they would need something that makes it easy to hide so that no one sees you. Maybe some sort of camouflage."

JT sat up straight and looked Micky directly in the eyes. "That's it!"

"What? Camouflage? That's already been invented."

"Yeah, but I'm not thinking about any old camouflage. I'm thinking about the ultimate camouflage."

"The ultimate camouflage?"

"Exactly. What do so many spaceships from

their cheesy movies have so that the enemy can't see them?"

Micky furrowed her brow. "Something to make them invisible, right?"

JT grabbed Micky's hands. "A cloaking device."

"There's no way. They would have to find a way to bend light around the whole car."

"Ha! They've already invented time travel. We invented hover technology, and we're trying to teleport something. I'm pretty sure a cloaking device isn't out of the realm of possibility here."

"That would definitely make it safer to go back in time, but do you really think that's what they're working on?"

JT closed her eyes and tried to remember back to last summer. She had been sitting near Jax in church and a note with Izzy's handwriting was on top of his Bible. *What did it say?* She focused harder and suddenly the words popped into her mind. "Ask about Dr. Aoki's cloak."

"Huh? Girl, what are you talking about?" Micky asked.

"At church Jax had a note from Izzy that had those words on it. I was going to look it up when I got home, but I forgot all about it until now."

JT walked over to Micky's computer and typed "Dr. Aoki cloak" into the search engine. "Here, this guy is one of the leading researchers in cloaking theory." She clicked on another link and quickly scanned the article. "It says that he has successfully made a coin appear to be invisible."

"And, look at this." Micky pointed to the area of the screen that displayed a brief bio of the scientist. "He's about the same age as Jax's dad and they graduated from the same school. I bet they know each other, and the guys got some advice from him."

"Bingo." JT grinned. "Looks like we might have some competition after all."

"Only if they pull it off," Micky said.

JT walked back and sat in front of MAT. "Yeah, well they aren't the only ones with work to do."

Six

"Now open your eyes," Jax said. "Check it out."

Izzy opened his eyes and stared at the seemingly empty spot on the table in front of him. "Where is it? Are you joking?"

"Nope. No joke."

"That's incredible! How did you get it to work?"

"Look closely," Jax said. "It didn't actually disappear, but at first glance it seems to. Try to look through it, and you'll see the background is a bit distorted."

Izzy eyes were wide open. "I can't believe it." He moved his hand toward the spot where the model car had sat just moments ago. His fingers vanished when they neared the project, then a pocket of air seemed to ripple as his hand bumped the invisible car. He clicked the switch in his hand and the plastic model and his fingers seemed to materialize on the workbench in Jax's garage.

In the past year, the Thompsons had hired a construction team to expand the garage so that Jax and his father could both use the place as a lab. It was now more than twice as large and contained some fairly advanced equipment the boys weren't allowed to use without Dr. Thompson's supervision.

"Pretty sweet, huh?" Jax asked.

"That's a major understatement. And we don't

have any top secret power sources this year." He looked up at Jax. "We're going to win."

Jax nodded, a smug smile on his lips. "The girls were pretty impressive last year, but I don't think there's any way they can top this. Plus, I got the impression from JT that they're having several problems."

"Oh, yeah? What sort of problems?"

He shrugged. "She hasn't said anything, but in class today I could tell she was frustrated with whatever they were working on."

Izzy clicked the switch on again and whistled as the car disappeared. "So it all came down to perfecting the field's settings?"

"Yeah, my dad helped me with it last night after you left. He called Dr. Aoki for advice and realized that we hadn't properly scaled our settings for an object of this size. So once we adjusted the electromagnetic field, the cloak worked perfectly."

"Seriously? How could we miss that?"

Jax laughed. "Sometimes it's the little things that get overlooked."

Shaking his head, Izzy turned off the device and spun to face the time machine. "So how are we supposed to get this thing to disappear?"

"My dad didn't think it would be too hard." Jax picked up the model car and touched a tiny metallic rod attached to the door. "We'll need to install a dozen rods like this one to generate the proper field. Of course, they'll be much bigger; each will be about three inches long. My dad is having one of his guys make them, so we should have the parts tomorrow. He's going to install some on that." Jax nodded to the shiny yellow Camaro parked next to the time machine.

Izzy chuckled. "It's a good thing your dad plans on time travelling by himself. Can you imagine the girls squished in the back?"

"Yeah, I don't think they'd like that."

Turning back to the model, Izzy held it up and peered into the interior. "Did you stick a camera in this thing to determine if a person can see out of a cloaked vehicle?"

"Yep, we tried it last night. We were right. Once the cloak is turned on, you can't see through the field at all. So if we were inside the car and we turned it on, then we wouldn't see anything outside. No one can see in, and no one can see out."

"But only the edge of the field is cloaked? The whole interior of the model didn't disappear, right?"

Jax set the model on the table. "That's right. Thankfully, we'll be able to see all the controls and each other."

"Okay, so we just need to stick some cameras outside, and run the feed to the screen, right?"

"Yeah, that would work, but we've got something better in mind."

Jax heard the security system's beep indicating the door's access code had been successfully entered. "Perfect timing." He glanced over as the door opened and his father walked in. "Hey, Dad, how was work?"

Dr. Thompson set a package on the edge of the bench. "It was fine, but busy. I was trying to get everything in order for that trip to DC this weekend." He put an arm around Jax and gave him a quick side hug.

"DC?" Izzy asked. "Why are you going there Dr. T.?"

"I told you before," Jax said. "He's getting that award from the president."

Izzy stared at Dr. Thompson. "Wait. *The* president?"

Jax pretended to look annoyed and sighed. "Now I see how much you pay attention to what I say."

Izzy's eyes widened, "When you said Washington, I thought you meant Washington State. Wow, that's awesome. Congratulations."

"Thanks, Isaiah. So what do you think of your project now?" Dr. Thompson pointed to the model car.

"It's amazing."

Jax motioned to the box his father had set down. "So is that what I think it is?"

"Yeah, what'd you bring us?" Izzy asked, rubbing his hands together and bouncing like a kid on Christmas.

"Oh, nothing too important." Dr. Thompson grinned. "Just a specialized camera that will allow us to see out of the vehicle when the cloaking technology is turned on."

"Cool. That's for us, right?" Izzy asked.

"I don't remember you guys giving me four thousand dollars recently, so, no, I don't think so." He shook his head and laughed. "This little baby is going in my car."

Izzy turned and looked at the new Camaro-turned-time-machine sitting next to the old car. "Ah, come on, Dr. Thompson, couldn't you wait for a buy one, get one deal?"

"That may be an awfully long wait, but since your rods aren't finished yet, you guys can help me install it."

Jax grabbed the box and cautiously pulled out an odd-looking device. "So this camera will really record 360 degrees at once?"

"It will do that and more. It can actually record up and down at the same time that it records all four directions."

Izzy examined the multi-camera. "I can't wait to see it."

He opened the door of the newer time machine and pointed to the dash. "But what good will all those angles be on this little seven inch monitor? You'd have to toggle through several screens just to see in each direction."

Jax grinned and motioned with his eyes for Izzy to wait for the answer from his dad.

"Didn't Jax tell you?"

"Tell me what?"

"Isaiah, that little screen is only for viewing what's underneath the car when hovering. I've already installed a separate camera for that. The windows were specially made to double as monitors. This camera will actually transmit the signal directly to each of the windows and the sunroof, so it will be just like you're looking out the windows.

"No way," Izzy said.

Jax nodded. "Yes way."

"You guys may have built the world's first time machine," Jax's father said, "but I'm going to be the first to time travel in style."

"What are we waiting for?" Jax asked. "Let's hook it up."

For the next hour, Izzy helped Jax and his dad install the new camera. They were nearly finished mounting it when Izzy received a message.

Izzy checked his phone, then returned it to his pocket. "Hey, I'd love to stick around and get this working, but my mom needs help with something at home. I'll stop by tomorrow to see it."

"Alright, see ya later," Jax said.

"Good night, Isaiah. Thanks for your help on this."

"You're welcome, Dr. T. Thanks for letting me

work on it. It's gonna be awesome. See ya, Jax." Izzy turned and left the garage.

"He's a good kid," Jax's father said. "You two work well together."

Jax tightened a screw on the enclosure they had built for the camera to protect it from the elements when it wasn't in use. "Yeah, well, we've been through a lot. He's been my best friend since seventh grade. It's a good thing, too. We need to win the science fair this year, so we really have to be on the same page."

His father smiled as he handed him another screw and held the camera's retractable mount in place. "What? You mean you aren't going to let your girlfriend win it again this year?"

"Dad." Jax blushed. "JT's not my girlfriend. At least not in the way you think."

Dr. Thompson held up both hands in a gesture of surrender. "Okay, okay." He paused, then asked, "So what is going on with the two of you? It's obvious that you like each other. How come you don't take her out on dates?"

Jax made sure the mounting post was secure before setting down the screwdriver on the work table. He sat down, knowing that this conversation might take a little while. Having his dad back was a dream come true, and Jax loved that he now took an interest in his personal life, but he didn't know if he could make him understand the change in his convictions since becoming a Christian. He said a quick prayer and took a deep breath, "Because we agreed not to date."

A rare expression appeared on his father's face. He looked confused. "Why?"

Earlier in the year, Jax had struggled to explain his position on this subject to Izzy, a fellow believer. He wasn't sure how to explain it to someone like his father. He shrugged one shoulder. "Why should we date?"

His dad let out a little laugh, but he still wore a confused look. "Because that's what a guy and girl usually do when they like each other. It gives you an opportunity to get to know each other better."

"Yeah, I know that's what most people do, but what's the point? I mean, we can still get to know each other by hanging out the way we do."

"So are you saying that you've never even kissed her?"

Jax shook his head. "No, she kissed me on the cheek once." He grinned and blushed slightly. "I know this is going to sound strange, but she apologized for it a few days later."

"Why?" Confusion had given way to incredulity on his dad's face.

"Because she was afraid she was giving me the wrong impression. She explained that she wasn't willing to base our relationship on the physical stuff."

"Jax, I don't mean to get too personal, but there's nothing wrong with kissing."

"It isn't that there's something necessarily wrong with it, but we talked about it and decided that it's something we wanted to save for our future spouses."

"Okay, but what if *she* is your future wife?"

"But I don't know if she will be. She may become somebody else's wife, and I might be somebody else's future husband." Jax took a deep breath, sat up straight, and looked his dad in the eyes. "Dad, did you ever date girls before you met Mom?"

Dr. Thompson put his hands in his pockets. "There were a few. But to be honest, I was always more interested in being in the lab before your mom came along."

"But did you ever do anything on those dates that at the time you thought was okay, but now you wish you could take back?"

His dad broke eye contact and gently kicked a piece of scrap metal toward the recycle bin. "Yeah, I did. I guess I see your point. But you can still go on dates without doing that sort of thing."

"I know we can, but…" He paused, embarrassed.

"But it's hard because you want to do that sort of thing." There was a new note of respect in his dad's voice, though Jax didn't look up.

His gaze still fixed on the floor, Jax nodded. "It's safer to avoid temptation."

There was a pause, then his dad briefly rested a hand on his shoulder. "You're one smart kid, Jax."

Jax took another deep breath. "Anyway, so that's why we always have other people, like Izzy and Micky, with us when we do things together. When I watch movies at her place, it's always with at least one of her parents."

An awkward silence hung in the air for a few moments. Jax stood and picked up the screwdriver again. "Besides, if we do end up getting married, at least I know we're already great friends."

Dr. Thompson grabbed the installation manual and searched for the appropriate page. "Son, I know I don't tell you this enough, but I'm really proud of you. You're a much better kid than I ever was."

"Thanks, Dad. Maybe it's because I have great parents."

His dad looked up and smiled.

Seven

"Sure beats sitting in class, doesn't it?" Izzy asked.

Jax nodded. "Skip day rules." He felt the butterflies in his stomach intensify as the train neared the top of the first climb. He looked out over the park at the other roller coasters with their brightly colored peaks and loops. Far beyond them, the Pacific Ocean stretched until it melded with the clear blue sky, making it impossible to determine where one ended and the other began. JT was in the car in front of him, clinging to the safety bar. Micky sat next to her, holding her hands high in the air.

The roller coaster slowly inched toward the apex. *Click, clack, click, clack.* Jax and Izzy raised their hands above their heads just as their cart tilted down. "Here we go!" The car raced down the 250-foot drop at a blistering speed, and Jax screamed in delight, his heart in his throat.

Three loops, a couple of corkscrew turns, and a minute later, the Trolley of Terror stopped at the station. After the safety bar retracted, Jax unstrapped himself and jumped out. "That was awesome. Let's do it again."

"I'm in," Izzy said.

Micky stumbled while climbing out as her foot caught the edge of the car, but she quickly recovered. "Me too."

JT slowly exited the coaster with one hand on her stomach. "Count me out. I think that first drop was too much for me."

"Come on, girl," Micky said. "We need an even number."

"I'm sorry. I really don't feel up to it."

Jax walked through the exit gate. "Well, we can find another ride and do this one later."

"But we're already here." Micky pointed to the entrance of the coaster. "And there's hardly anyone in line right now."

"Danielle can go with you."

Jax spun around to see who had spoken. Mara and Danielle stood nearby. Mara's expression was similar to JT's.

"I don't think I could handle another run right now either," Mara said. She looked at JT. "We could just hang around here while they ride again."

"Is that okay with you?" Micky asked.

"Yeah, that sounds like a good idea," JT said. "Have fun."

"We'll meet you back here when it's done." Jax clapped Izzy's shoulder. "Let's go."

"How about that bench over there?" JT asked. "It's in the shade."

Mara pushed her sunglasses to the top of her head. "Looks good."

The two girls sat on the bench. JT took a deep breath and leaned her head back as she tried to calm her stomach.

"Are you guys having fun so far?" Mara asked.

"The guys have been looking forward to this all year, and they're having a great time." Ever since the Gold Rush Theme Park opened, the juniors and seniors of Silicon Valley Prep had taken a school-sponsored skip day in the spring to enjoy a day away from the classroom.

"But you're not?"

"I am." She shrugged. "I'm just not a big fan of roller coasters, and I'm definitely not going on that one again. How about you?"

Mara rested her arm on the back of the bench. "The same. It's a lot better than being in class, but I still have to write a report for Mr. Li dealing with the physics of the ride of my choice."

"Hmm. Glad I took his class last year." JT managed a small smile. "We didn't have to do that."

"Yeah, I wish I had taken it last year too." Mara's voice was barely audible. She looked as if she were deep in thought for a few seconds. Then she turned to JT with a concerned look. "You know, I really appreciate how you answered those questions about the Bible back at the cabin."

Although she still felt a bit nauseated, JT pulled her feet up on the bench and turned to face her friend. "Thanks. I'm always happy to talk about the Bible."

"Good, because I was hoping to talk to you about it some more." She stared at her feet. "I've always known that you were a Christian, but I've never met someone who takes it so seriously. And you actually study the Bible. I mean, your faith isn't just something you do on the side, but it seems like it's a part of who you are." She looked up at JT. "I really respect you for that, even though I don't have the same beliefs. It's refreshing."

JT blushed slightly.

"Well, it made me wonder why that stuff is so important to you. So I found my grandma's old Bible sitting on our bookshelf, and I started reading."

The sick feeling lessened as excitement began to fill JT's mind. "Cool. What did you read?"

"I was basically just skimming it from the beginning, but I kind of got stuck in Leviticus. What's the deal with all those sacrifices and rituals that they had to do? There sure was a lot of blood." Mara made a face. "Your church isn't like that, is it?"

JT smiled. "No, my church isn't like that, and I don't know of any that are. I'm happy to say the New Testament changed all that. It's important to understand why those sacrifices were required, though. The purpose wasn't just to kill a lot of animals. It was so the people could realize the seriousness of their sins."

Mara furrowed her brow. "And how does killing animals accomplish that?"

"Did you read the first few chapters of Genesis?"

"Not really," Mara said, shaking her head. "I skimmed that, too. I saw that it was about God creating everything, but I had already heard about that, and I wanted to get to something more interesting. What does creation have to do with all the sacrifices?"

"The Bible tells us that when God made everything, it was perfect. There was no death or disease of any kind. But then the first man and woman, Adam and Eve, decided to disobey God."

"That's when they ate the apple, right?"

"Uh, sort of. The Bible never says that it was an apple. They ate the fruit from the tree of the knowledge of good and evil—we don't know what it looked like. That's another one of those areas where people don't read carefully or they just repeat what they've heard, like we saw with David and Goliath." JT paused as a train full of screaming people whipped overhead.

Mara motioned to the ride with her eyes. "I'm glad we're not on that."

JT's stomach churned as she watched the cars zip past. "Me too." She waited until the noise subsided. "Where were we?"

"You were explaining why there were so many sacrifices."

"Oh, yeah, that's right. God told Adam that the penalty for disobedience was death."

"Whoa, isn't that a bit harsh? Just for eating a piece of fruit?" Mara asked.

"That's the whole point. We tend to think that disobeying isn't all that serious. Instead of looking at the wrong action and trying to judge whether it's really serious or not, we need to remember that every sin is an act of rebellion against God, who is infinitely pure. Also, Adam and Eve were given a perfect environment. They didn't have the tendency to sin like we do, and they *still* chose to rebel."

"So you're saying that the penalty is harsh because of who the sin is committed against?"

"That's right, and because God is the Creator, He has the right to set the rules and carry out the punishment. So He would have been completely justified in putting Adam and Eve to death right away." JT gestured with her hands. "They would still eventually die for their sin, but God is merciful. The Bible says that He made coats of skin to clothe Adam and Eve. That means He must have killed an animal or two, setting the example for all those sacrifices you read about in Leviticus. Those weren't done because God enjoys death, but because the penalty for sin is death—only God allowed animals to be killed instead of people. The death of so many animals would be a constant reminder of just how serious sin is to God."

Mara looked confused. "Okay, so they reminded people how serious sin is, but did the sacrifices do anything else? I mean, some of the ancient religions that I studied taught that their gods would be appeased when the people sacrificed to them. Was God happy with them when they sacrificed the animals?"

JT took a sip of her bottled water. "I have never given much thought to the sacrifices in other religions before. That's true that those people did all sorts of things to make their god or gods happy. But the sacrifices that the Israelites offered were different; they couldn't take away sins. Instead, when the people sacrificed animals, they demonstrated their obedience to God's command and their trust that He would fulfill His promises."

"Promises? Like what?"

Another train full of screaming passengers roared by, causing JT to pause before answering. "There were a lot of them. But the biggest promise had to do with the sacrifice that God Himself would make."

"Are you talking about Jesus dying on the Cross?"

JT smiled. "Exactly. Those sacrifices described in the Old Testament pointed forward to what Jesus would do on the Cross. Since animal sacrifices could never take away our sins, we needed a perfect person to be our substitute. So that's what Jesus did. By dying on the Cross in our place, He took the punishment that we deserve. Then He rose from the dead three days later to show His power over death, and to give the hope of eternal life. Those who turn from their sins and believe in Him are forgiven and will go to heaven when they die."

"So you're saying that a person just needs to believe in Jesus to go to heaven? Don't you think that sounds…" Mara looked as if she was searching for the right word. "It all just sounds too easy."

"What do you mean?"

"In other religions you have to follow a bunch of rules to get to heaven or paradise or wherever, but you're saying that Christianity isn't like that."

"I guess in that sense, you could call it easy. But that's one of the things that sets Christianity apart from manmade religions. It isn't about what you do for your god or gods; it's about what God has already done for you." JT stretched her legs out and then crossed them. "Think about it like this: God is perfect, and the only way we can be with Him is to be perfect. But we've all done wrong things before, right?"

"Yeah, but I'm not a bad person. I'd like to think I've done more good than bad," Mara said.

"Maybe you have, but that doesn't really matter." JT paused for a moment, casting around for the words to help Mara understand. *Lord, please help me explain this to her in the right way, and please open her mind to the truth.*

Her gaze landed on a nearby concession stand. "Imagine you were arrested for robbing that ice cream cart, but you've never broken the law at any other time. When you stand before the judge, you can't really say, 'Your honor, I know I'm guilty of stealing, but I've never done it before, so I think you should let me go.' If he's a good judge, he won't let you off the hook. You've broken the law, and there are consequences for doing that."

Mara scratched her head. "So God is like the judge in your analogy. But I thought you said God was merciful. Why doesn't He count the good stuff you've done?"

"It isn't like a scale, where the good has to outweigh the bad." JT thought for a moment as she waited for the screams and roar of the ride to subside. "We've all broken His laws, and because God is the perfect Judge, He has to punish sin. It isn't a matter of trying to cover up our sins by doing good deeds. Those may look impressive, but if you still have sins on your account when you stand before Him, God must judge you. Your sins have to be removed." She leaned forward, gesturing with her hands. "But here's the great thing: Jesus paid for our sins on the Cross, and all who receive that payment on their behalf will have their sins taken away."

For a time Mara said nothing. Then she took a deep breath. "Okay, but what about all the other people in the world who sincerely follow their own religions?"

"It doesn't matter how sincere a person is if they're wrong. Just like you can sincerely believe you solved a math problem, but if you have the wrong answer, it doesn't matter that you fully believe it to be correct. Those other religions don't offer forgiveness and they teach that a person can earn their own salvation by being good enough."

"Do you believe that they all go to hell then?" Mara cocked her head, and JT could see her distaste for the idea written on her face.

"I would say that if a person dies without being forgiven of their sins, then yes, they will have to pay the penalty for their own sins for eternity. That may sound harsh, but since God is a just judge, He can't let people off the hook." JT clasped her hands together. "Mara, you need to decide how you will respond to what Jesus has done for you. You can ignore Him and keep trying on your own to be good enough, hoping that will offset the bad. Or you can call on Him and ask Him to save you."

Mara sat quietly for a moment. "I don't know. I mean, it's a lot to take in. I get what you're saying, and it makes a lot of sense when you say it, but I need some time to think it through."

"I understand. I'm not trying to pressure you into it, but please don't put it off and ignore it. Think about what we've talked about and keep reading your Bible. Remember, avoiding the decision is the same as making a decision." JT saw her friends returning from the ride. "Call me any time if you have questions, and I'll do my best to help."

Mara smiled and gave her a quick hug. "Thanks."

"You guys missed out. That thing is awesome," Jax said.

"Once was more than enough for me," Mara said.

"Me too," JT said.

"Well, it's your loss." Jax looked at JT. "Are you up for some lunch?"

JT grabbed her second slice of pizza from the middle of the table and sprinkled parmesan cheese on it, carefully holding the container's lid with her fingertips so that it wouldn't fall off after she had loosened it.

Izzy snorted. "You Midwesterners put cheese on everything."

"Well, it is pizza. Besides, everything's better with cheese on it." JT smiled, thinking about how often her dad had said those words when she was a young kid growing up in Wisconsin. "You should try it."

"No thanks. It's already got enough cheese," Izzy said.

"But it's good, right?"

"Yeah, because it already has the right amount."

"That's where you're wrong. More will only make it taste better. Are you scared to try it?"

"Here, let me try it." Jax said as he reached for the parmesan.

JT elbowed Micky to get her attention.

Jax tipped the glass container over his slice of pizza. As he shook the bottle, the lid slid off and the cheese dumped all over his plate. JT, Micky, and Izzy erupted in laughter, while Jax turned red and looked around to see if anyone else had witnessed the prank. He shook his head and flashed a toothy grin. "Nice one, JT. I can't believe I fell for that."

When she finished giggling, JT grabbed her plate and held it out to Jax. "Here, I'll take yours, and you can try it with"—she glanced at Izzy and smirked—"the *right* amount."

Jax accepted her offer. "Thanks. I'll get you back someday. Maybe soon."

"Okay, changing topics here," Izzy said. "How are things coming on your project? Have you finished it?"

JT set her drink down. "We've still got a few kinks to work out, but don't worry, we'll still have it done in time to whup you guys again."

"We told you before, you might want to prepare to be content with second place," Jax said.

Micky bumped JT with her knee and winked. "You guys really think your cloaking device is going to be good enough to beat us?"

The boys looked taken aback. Izzy gave Micky a blank stare, his mouth slightly open, while Jax let out a nervous laugh. "What are you talking about?"

JT looked at Micky. "Bingo. I knew it."

"A cloaking device?" Jax asked. He turned to Izzy. "Why didn't we think of that?"

"Nice try, Thompson," Micky said. "We know that's what you guys are up to."

"Yeah, how's Dr. Aoki?" JT asked.

Jax slapped both hands on the table and glared at Izzy. "Did you tell them?"

"Hey, don't look at me," Izzy said. He turned to the girls. "How did you know?"

"We have our ways." Micky smiled and tossed her ponytail over her shoulder.

JT arched her eyebrows coyly while the guys spluttered, demanding to know how they had found out.

Finally Jax gave in. "Okay, well you know what we're building, so why don't you tell us what you're working on?"

"Not a chance," Micky said. "But I can tell you that the only hope you have of beating us is if you cloak our project so the judges don't see it."

EIGHT

Pastor Carl pulled a folded piece of paper from his pocket. "We received this note from Pastor Rich this week, and I wanted to share it with you."

To my family in Mountain View,
I am having a wonderful time doing the work over here, and I'm meeting so many new friends. They are excited that I am here. I miss you very much, and am looking forward to seeing you all again in a few short months.

"For those of you who are new, Pastor Rich is our full-time youth pastor, and he's doing some mission work in the Middle East. The work he's talking about is distributing Bibles in places where God's Word isn't allowed. That's why his e-mail is a bit cryptic."

He set the note on the podium. "Remember that we're having a game night on Friday beginning at seven. Bring a friend."

JT grabbed her notebook and Bible off the floor before standing. *I can't take much more of this.* She looked around and saw Jax running for the game tables. Izzy had already joined a small group gathered around the interim youth pastor, and Micky was chatting with some friends. She felt someone grab her shoulder. Turning, she saw her friend Emma and gave her a quick hug.

Emma flashed a sympathetic smile. "Another dud, huh?"

JT made sure no one else was listening. "It was awesome to hear from Pastor Rich, but I really miss his teaching. Even if some of the kids thought he was boring, at least he taught the Bible every week."

"Only three more months, right?"

"Until Pastor Rich gets back?"

Emma nodded.

"I think so. I just hope I can make it until then."

"I know what you mean." Emma glanced at the group around Pastor Carl and leaned in close to JT. "I talked to my dad about it, and he said that it's tough to handle these things. Most of the kids really like Pastor Carl, and the group *is* growing."

JT held her arms out. "But what good is it if they aren't learning anything and aren't even hearing the gospel? It's not that I don't like the guy, but..."

"But what?"

"Nothing. My mom told me to make sure I don't harbor any bitterness toward Pastor Carl, so maybe we should change the subject." She looked at the ground. "I just can't wait until Pastor Rich comes back."

"Well, look at it this way. If he can spend half

a year risking his life to get Bibles out there, then we can survive for a few more months."

JT smiled and hugged her friend. "Thanks. I needed that."

"Me too. I have to get going. I'll see you Sunday," Emma said before walking toward the exit.

Several minutes later, JT walked through the parking lot with Micky, Jax, and Izzy. She wanted to join their conversation about the rafting trip, but was still distracted with the direction, or non-direction, of the youth group.

When they reached Jax's car, he looked at JT. "You're awfully quiet. What were you and Emma talking about?"

She wanted to ignore the question, but all eyes were on her. *How am I going to explain this?*

"It looked like it was something serious," Jax said.

She smiled and nudged him with her shoulder, trying to lighten the mood. "How would you know? You and Bobby were busy playing foosball."

Jax smiled. "It doesn't take all my focus to dominate." His smile faded. "But seriously, I know you better than that. Something's bothering you."

She gave him the "drop it" look, but he didn't get the message.

"So what's going on?"

She glanced from Jax to the others and back, then sighed. "It's about the direction of the youth group. Ever since Pastor Rich left, it hasn't been the same."

"Yeah, it's a lot more fun," Micky said.

"That's—" JT began, but Izzy interrupted.

"Nothing against Pastor Rich, but Micky's right, Pastor Carl is a lot cooler. Just look at how many new people have been coming since he's been here."

JT bit her bottom lip and looked at Jax for support.

"Are you saying you don't like Pastor Carl?" Jax asked. "Because I think he's great."

"No, I don't have anything against him personally." JT struggled to find words that wouldn't come across as bitter or judgmental. "I just don't like the changes that have been made."

"What changes?" Izzy asked.

"Look, I'm glad you guys like coming, and I'm not trying to be a wet blanket spoiling your fun." She held up her Bible. "But think about it. When was the last time we actually studied this in youth group?"

After a prolonged silence, Micky said, "Just last week. Remember, he had us find that passage in Matthew?"

"That's right," Izzy said, but he looked relieved that Micky had come up with something.

"Yeah, we looked it up and he read two verses," JT said before setting her Bible on the car. "Then he went on and told a couple of funny stories and never talked about those verses again."

"He still teaches us about the Bible though," Micky said.

Jax leaned against the car. "And he does it in a fun way. That's probably why so many new people have been coming. I mean, don't get me wrong; I love Pastor Rich. But I think Pastor Carl's doing a great job filling in."

JT studied each of them in turn. "Is that really the way you guys feel?"

They nodded.

"Then here's a question. Can you tell me one thing about the Bible that you've learned from Pastor Carl? Jax?"

Jax tapped his foot on the ground as he searched for an answer. "I don't know. I guess there's just a lot of little things."

"Such as?"

He shoved his hands into his pockets. "Well, like last week, he talked about how God made everyone for a specific purpose."

"And that's something new for you?" JT asked.

"Not really. But what's wrong with it?"

"Nothing. It's not necessarily that he's teaching something false, but there's hardly any depth to any of it."

"But don't you think that's better for some of the newcomers?" Jax asked.

JT paused for a moment to think through her answer before speaking. "Last year when you were mad at God because of what happened to your dad, would it have helped you if I told you that God made you for a specific purpose?"

He shook his head. "No. I think I would have just gotten angrier. But that's sort of an extreme situation. Not everyone has to deal with the loss of their father at such a young age."

"No, but everyone has different struggles and questions. Little positive pep talks don't accomplish much. They don't go deep enough to deal with real issues."

JT waited for another question or objection, but no one spoke. Micky raised an eyebrow and shrugged.

"Look, I'm not saying that he isn't doing any good at all. I'm excited that there are so many new people coming, too, but if we give them a false view of Christianity, then I think we may be doing more harm than good."

"What do you mean?" Izzy asked, jumping up and sitting on the car's trunk. "How can it be harmful if they're hearing the truth, even if they aren't digging deep into the Bible?"

JT picked up her Bible and flipped through the pages until she found 2 Timothy 3:12. "Because if we're just telling everyone, 'Hey, Jesus loves you and has a wonderful plan for your life,' then we're giving them the wrong impression about Christianity. It's true that Jesus loves them, but the Bible says right here that 'all who desire to live godly in Christ Jesus will suffer persecution.'"

She set the Bible back down. "Pastor Carl's type of teaching is short-sighted. If these new people think Christianity is all about fun and games, and having a better life now, then they are being misled. The Bible promises that we'll be persecuted. Our problems won't go away, but God can give us the strength to get through tough times, and He can even give us joy in our struggles. What's going to happen to these guys when times get tough? Will they just say, 'Oh well, I guess this Christianity thing didn't work,' and walk away?"

"Don't you think you're overreacting a bit?" Izzy asked. "You have to get people in the door before you can hit 'em with the heavy stuff."

"But the problem is that whatever it takes to get someone in the door is what it takes to keep them coming back. So if it takes fun and games to bring people in, then most of the time, it's going to take more fun and games to keep them there. But if they are coming because they want to hear the truth, then we need to keep on teaching the truth." JT rubbed her forehead. "Besides, isn't that a bait-and-switch—to lure them with fun and games, but then alter the message? Most people won't stick around once the switch is made because that's not what they signed up for."

"Those are good points, and I get what you're saying," Izzy said. "But I still think you're making too much of it."

"Yeah, besides, I like that things aren't always just black and white with him, like they usually are with you," Micky said. "No offense."

JT looked from one of her friends to another, a little taken aback. She had thought they would see her way of thinking once she explained it, but instead they turned things back on her. "What do you mean?"

"Sorry, I'm not trying to be rude"—Micky crossed her arms—"but it seems like things are your way or the highway when it comes to the Bible. Can't you see how narrow-minded that makes you sound?"

JT bit her lip. "I'm not saying that it's my way or the highway," she began carefully, "just that there is only *one* right way to interpret it. I know that I'm wrong at times—I'm a finite being; I only have a finite understanding, and we're talking about the infinite here—but that doesn't mean we can make the Bible say whatever we want or that it can have different meanings for different people. We have to be careful to let the author, God, tell us what He means, not the other way around."

"Okay, so how do you know when you are doing it right?" Micky asked. "You told me the Bible clearly teaches that God made everything in six twenty-four hour days, but Pastor Carl said that isn't necessarily true."

JT's eyes widened. "What? When did he say that?"

"I asked him about it a few weeks ago. You know that I've never agreed with you on the age of the earth. I knew that Pastor Rich agreed with you, but I wanted to know what another pastor thought about it."

"And what did he say?"

"He said that he thought God probably did everything in six days, like you believe, but he didn't think it was a big deal one way or the other. He said that there are a lot of sincere Christians out there who believe God used billions of years to make everything. And some even believe that God used evolution."

JT's frustration with Pastor Carl rose another notch. She could feel her face getting warmer but tried to remain calm.

As if he could read her emotions, Jax placed his hand on her shoulder. "Micky, don't you see the problems with that type of thinking?"

Micky shrugged and shook her head. "Not really, it makes a lot of sense to me, and I think it even demonstrates some humility on his part by admitting there may be other good points of view out there."

"Hold on," JT broke in. She could hear the edge in her own voice but found she could no longer completely suppress her frustration. "It's actually prideful—the *opposite* of humility—to deny the clear words of the Bible, because then you are putting your own ideas in there and putting yourself in God's place. I'll admit that there are some passages that aren't very clear, and in those areas we need to be very cautious. But there are many areas where it is clear, like creation and the age of the earth."

"And the point isn't that there are sincere Christians that believe those things. There are," Jax said. "But we need to ask, 'What did God really say about it?' The Bible is consistent in teaching that God made everything in six days, that there was no death or suffering before Adam's sin, and that there was a worldwide Flood. If we tell people they don't have to believe those things in Genesis, why would they believe the stuff in Matthew, Mark, Luke, and John?"

Micky looked at Izzy, who seemed quite content to remain silent, and then at Jax. "Of course you're going to take her side."

Jax sighed. "Come on, Micky. Give me some credit. It isn't about taking sides. It's about accepting or rejecting what the Bible teaches. You can't pick and choose which parts you want to believe."

"I'm not saying that. I'm just asking how you

can know if your interpretation of the Bible is right."

"But this isn't a place that's open to interpretation," JT said, shaking off Jax's hand as he tried to squeeze her shoulder. "The Bible clearly says, 'So the *evening* and the *morning* were the first *day*.'"

Micky pursed her lips, eyeing JT coldly. "Frankly, I think it's refreshing that Pastor Carl is willing to think outside the box."

JT crossed her arms on the top of the car and buried her face in them. After a moment, she looked up. "Well, if the box is the Bible, then he's definitely thinking outside it. Nobody is saying that a person can't be a Christian if they believe in evolution or billions of years. What we're saying is that it comes down to whether you are going to believe God's Word or man's word. In Matthew 19, Jesus said that Adam and Eve were created *at the beginning*. It is short-sighted to tell people that they can stick their own ideas into the Bible rather than just accepting what it says. And let's be honest, the major reason so many people try to reinterpret Genesis is because of what most scientists believe. If that's your approach, then where does it stop? After Genesis? The New Testament? Should we deny Christ's virgin birth, miracles, and Resurrection? After all, most scientists do."

"But maybe you're taking what it says too literally. Pastor Carl said that you don't have to.

Maybe the beginning of Genesis is just meant to be poetic or symbolic or something."

Jax joined Izzy on the trunk of the car. "I thought about that too, so I asked Pastor Rich about it. He said Genesis is written as historical narrative, just like Exodus, Leviticus, Numbers, and so on. That style of writing should be interpreted in a straightforward manner by trying to understand the plain meaning, while still allowing for some figures of speech. But poetry is very different. It uses different verb forms and a ton of figurative language. It's usually pretty easy to tell the difference."

Micky pursed her lips. "Yeah, but even with narrative, you still don't have to take everything literally."

JT stood up straight. "That's true. Like Jax said, there are figures of speech, but words have meaning. While we have been talking we've been interpreting each other's words in a straightforward manner. You haven't tried to make my words, or Jax's words, poetic, and we haven't done that to you. Why? Because it's usually not hard to tell when someone is using literal or figurative language. If we tried to communicate the way you're saying we should interpret Genesis 1, then we'd never understand each other."

After a few seconds of silence, Izzy cleared his throat and slid off the trunk. "I don't know about you guys, but I *literally* have a backpack full of homework to do tonight. Maybe we can continue this conversation later."

Jax laughed, but Micky turned away unsmiling and got into the car without a word. Remorse washed over JT. *I shouldn't have gotten so worked up. Is it me, God? Is my black-and-white attitude keeping Micky from You?*

She looked up at the stars as Jax and Izzy climbed into the front seats, and suddenly she knew the answer. Whatever still stood between Micky and God, her defense of the truth wasn't one of them. *Still, God, please help me always to be gentle. I know the truth matters…but help me not to use it as a blunt object.*

NINE

"Thanks for driving. Even though it sounds kind of lame, these reunions are usually pretty fun," Micky said before unbuckling and getting out of the car.

JT hid her purse under the seat, shut off the GPS, grabbed the keys, and soon joined Micky at the front of the car.

The drive had taken slightly less than the hour they expected, thanks to the traffic being surprisingly light. Neither she nor Micky had brought up the conversation they'd had after youth group. JT was content to leave it alone, devoting her attention instead to the landscape whizzing past and the fresh country air whipping at her hair through the open window. Being out of the city brought back memories from her childhood, even though everything here was brown and mountainous, whereas back where she grew up everything was green and flat or white and flat, depending on the season.

"Come on. I want you to meet my Aunt Nora." Micky grabbed JT's hand and ran toward the house. They soon reached the deck, where a brawny middle-aged man was dumping charcoal into a large grill. Beyond him, in an expansive yard, a couple of younger men were setting up a volleyball net, while an older man stacked wood near a fire pit.

"Hey, Uncle Steve," Micky said.

The man turned and set the bag down. A huge smile crossed his bearded face, and he held out his large hairy arms. "Micky. How's my favorite niece?"

She gave him a big hug. "This is my best friend, JT."

Steve shook JT's hand. "So you're the one that helped Micky win the science fair?"

"Yes sir," JT said.

"Sir?" He chuckled. "You can call me Uncle Steve."

"Okay. It's nice to meet you, Uncle Steve."

"The pleasure's all mine, JT. Well, you girls are here early. Nora's inside getting things ready."

"Cool," Micky said. "We'll go see if she needs any help."

Moments later, the girls entered the house through the patio door. A thin woman in a blue sundress stood at the counter with her back to them. She appeared to be chopping some vegetables. "Steve, don't forget to set up the chairs and tables in the garage."

Micky giggled. "Hi, Aunt Nora."

The woman spun around, and JT instantly recognized the family resemblance as the woman looked so much like Micky's dad. "Micky! I didn't expect you so soon." She set the knife down and gave Micky a hug. "And this must be JT."

"Yes, ma'am," JT said. She held out her hand, but Aunt Nora gave her a hug instead.

"It's so nice to meet you. Micky's told me all about your project last year."

"It's nice to meet you, and I've heard a lot about you, too."

"Aunt Nora, do you need help—"

"Micky's here!" a young girl shouted.

JT turned and saw two kids running down the hall toward them. She recognized the boy, who, if she remembered correctly, was about ten years old. The girl, who she had never met before, looked to be about seven.

Micky bent down and hugged them both at once. "JT, you know my brother, Andrew. This is my sister, Heather."

"Hey, guys." JT knew Heather was Micky's half-sister, her dad's daughter with his current wife. Andrew was her full brother, but he usually stayed with their father.

"Andrew, is Dad around?"

"He'll be here later. He had some work to do in town."

Micky mussed his hair. "Aunt Nora, do you need help with anything?"

"We've got all the food under control. Would you mind going to the garage and setting up the tables and chairs?"

"Sure, we'd be happy to."

"We'll help too," Andrew said.

A couple hours later, JT tossed her paper plate into the garbage can after polishing off one of Uncle Steve's delicious hamburgers with all the trimmings. She walked out of the garage and spotted Micky talking to her father by the fire pit. *She was right, this reunion is fun.*

JT swung her arms back and forth in front of and then behind her body, trying to loosen up a little for a few more games of volleyball. The clear blue sky served as a perfect backdrop for the large white salt-box home, complete with wraparound deck. She inhaled deeply. *It would be so nice to live out in the country again.* Several young adults and teenagers had gathered at the net, so JT headed toward it.

"JT!"

She stopped and saw Aunt Nora approaching with a man who looked like a larger, older version of Micky's father.

"I want you to meet someone. This is Micky's Uncle James."

James stood about six feet tall, and his light brown hair stuck out the sides and back of his ball cap. He held out his hand, his white teeth flashing in the sun as he smiled. "It's nice to meet you."

"It's nice to meet you, too," JT said, shaking his hand.

"JT is a Christian too," Nora said. "You two should get along well."

"Oh, really? Well, I'm glad to know Micky has a good influence in her life," James said.

I didn't realize there were any Christians in Micky's family. JT glanced at Micky and laughed. "Well, I try, but that girl needs serious help."

Nora and James laughed.

JT looked back at Micky. *She's been confronted with the truth so much. What's holding her back?*

"So where do you go to church?" James asked.

"Mountain View Bible Church. My dad is one of the elders there."

"I've never heard of that one, but I don't really make it up here much anymore. Is it new?"

JT placed her hand above her eyes to block the sunlight. "I don't think so. It was there when we moved here about five years ago, and our current pastor has been here longer than that. What church do you go to?"

"I go to a small church outside of Bakersfield."

"That's pretty far away, isn't it?" JT asked.

"Sure is. About four hours." He smiled, put an arm around Nora and squeezed her. "That's why I haven't been to one of Nora's parties in years."

Out of nowhere, Micky forcefully grabbed JT's arm. "We need to go now."

"What? Why?" JT asked, a little annoyed. "I thought we were going to play volleyball." She met Micky's eyes and blinked at the intensity she saw there. She could see her friend was serious. All annoyance gone, JT glanced at Micky's dad, who was attacking an ear of corn, seemingly unperturbed. "What's going on?"

Micky's nostrils flared. "We're leaving right now." She bared her teeth in a forced smile and said a perfunctory, "Good-bye, Aunt Nora" before turning and dragging JT toward the car.

JT looked back over her shoulder. "Um, I guess I need to go. It was so nice to meet you. Thank you for the great food." She pulled her arm away from Micky. "What is going on?"

Shaking her head, Micky pressed her lips into a thin line before muttering. "I'll tell you later. Let's just get out of here please."

"Are you feeling any better?" JT asked as she turned the car off in Micky's driveway.

Micky shook her head. "I'm just going to watch TV for a while."

JT was surprised to hear her respond. She had barely said a word the entire trip home, and JT had spent the drive silently trying to puzzle out what had upset her. "Okay, I need to come in and grab my stuff."

"That's fine."

As the girls entered the house, JT laid a hand

on Micky's arm. "Did I do something wrong?"

"No, it isn't you. I just need to lay down." They descended the basement stairs. Micky flipped the light switch and stopped.

JT couldn't believe her eyes. Their paperwork was strewn about the floor, as were bits and pieces of hardware. "What happened?"

Micky remained motionless.

JT looked at the table and couldn't see their project. Then she panned down. MAT was upside down on the floor. She ran to the device, knelt down, and carefully turned it over. The arm was snapped in two, a circuit board was splintered, and several frayed wires were exposed through a large crack in the front. She looked up at Micky, who was now standing next to her. "It's ruined."

Micky's eyes narrowed and burned with anger. Her face turned red as she let out a deep breath. "I'm going to kill them." She turned and ran toward the stairs.

"Wait!"

She reached the stairs and bounded up them three at a time.

JT sat silently, in shock. *How could this happen?* Tears built up in the corners of her eyes as she rose and gingerly placed the unit on the table. After a last look at the ruined teleporter, JT followed her friend up the stairs. Micky wasn't on the main floor, so JT ran outside. She saw Micky nearly a block away, running down the sidewalk.

"Micky!" She thought about chasing after her, either on foot or in the car, but decided that Micky just needed to blow off some steam. Hanging her head, JT turned back to the house. *I might as well clean up.*

TEN

Jax held up his index finger, interrupting Izzy's story. "Hold on a sec." He pulled out his phone, looked at the display, smiled, and then put it to his ear. "Hey, JT."

"What are you up to right now?"

"We just finished our project, so we're celebrating at Bits & Bytes—wait, you sound worried. Are you okay?"

"No, not really. Is Micky with you?" JT asked.

Jax shot a confused look at Izzy, who mouthed back something that Jax couldn't understand. "Uh, no. I thought she was with you. Weren't you guys going to her family reunion today?"

"We did, but we left after a couple of hours. She said she wasn't feeling well."

"So you tried her house, right?"

"That's where I am now. I've been waiting here since she left two hours ago, and I'm starting to get worried."

"What's going on?" Izzy asked.

Jax gave him a "not right now" look. "What do you mean 'left'? Where did she go?"

"I don't know. She was so mad that she just took off."

"Mad? At you?"

"No. Something happened at the reunion. I'm not sure what. Then when we got here and—"

Jax could hear her sniffling and waited a few seconds for her to finish her thought, but she didn't speak. "And what?"

"It's a long story. Would you guys mind if I dropped in for a bit?"

"Hold on." Jax looked at Izzy. "Do you mind if JT stops in?"

Izzy shook his head, still looking confused.

"No, that's fine. Actually, we're just getting ready to order. Did you want me to get you anything?"

"I don't know if I can eat much right now. Maybe just get me a side salad with ranch. I'll be there in a few minutes."

"Sounds good. Bye."

Jax put his phone back in his pocket and looked at Izzy.

"What was that all about?"

"I'm not sure. Sounds like something's going on with Micky. They left the reunion early because she wasn't feeling well. Then I guess Micky just took off when they got back to her place. That was about two hours ago. JT was waiting for her, but she still isn't back."

"What do you mean 'took off'? In her car?"

"She didn't say, and I didn't think to ask."

"She's probably just in one of her moods," Izzy said.

"I don't know. If that was it, I don't think JT

would have sounded so concerned." Out of the corner of his eye, Jax saw the waitress approaching their table.

"Are you guys ready to order?" she asked.

Jax and Izzy ordered their meals. The waitress had already turned around when Jax remembered he was supposed to order for JT. "Oh, and can I get a side salad with ranch dressing and a glass of water?"

"Sure, honey," she said as she scribbled on her pad. "I'll get this in right away."

Jax waited for her to leave. "So what do you think is going on with Micky?"

"I don't know. JT should be here soon. We can try to figure it out then." Izzy leaned back and put his hands behind his head. "It sure feels good to be done with our project with a couple of weeks to spare."

Jax laughed. "Yeah, not like last year. That was crazy."

"So now that we're done, we can take the car out again. Where do you want to go next?" He put his hands back on the table and leaned in.

Jax scooted forward and kept his voice down. "I'm not sure. Now that we'll be virtually invisible, it would be kind of fun to check out some of those dragon legends from history to see if the people were actually seeing dinosaurs. What about you?"

"That would be pretty cool, but not as cool as my idea."

Jax grew excited at the prospect of something better than dinosaurs. "What's your idea?"

Izzy looked around before speaking. "I was thinking we should take Micky back to witness the Resurrection of Christ."

Jax was stunned. It had never occurred to him that they could possibly go back to witness what he believed to be the single most important event in history. "Are you serious?"

Izzy nodded. "I can't even imagine what it would be like."

"Do you even think it would be okay to do something like that?"

"What do you mean?"

"I don't know. I just never thought of doing that." Jax tried to verbalize the objection, but he wasn't thinking straight. He knew the Bible said something about those who believed without seeing Christ being blessed, but he wasn't sure how that fit in with Izzy's proposition. Not to mention… He would know. Cloaked or not, Jesus would know they were there. What would that be like? To see Christ in the flesh? To know He knew you were watching Him?

Before Jax could put the pieces together, JT walked in.

"Hey, guys." She sat down next to Jax, her eyes

red and puffy. She had been crying recently.

Jax wanted to put his arm around her and comfort her, but thought better of it. He gave her a sympathetic look instead. "Heard anything from Micky?"

She looked down and shook her head.

"So what happened?" Izzy asked.

JT took a deep breath, folded her arms on the table and rested her chin on her wrist. She looked up at Izzy. "I don't really know. We were having a good time at the reunion, and then she just sort of snapped."

"What do you mean 'snapped'? You mean she yelled at you?"

"No, not like that. Out of the blue she said it was time to go and was very forceful about it. She said she wasn't feeling well, but I know there was more to it."

"Can you think of anything that might have happened to cause it?" Jax asked.

"I've been trying to think of something. We had played some volleyball with her cousins, and then we talked to some of her relatives. I got to meet one of her uncles, who said he was a Christian. I wanted to talk to him some more, but she yanked me away and said it was time to go."

"And she didn't say why?"

"No, she just said she didn't feel well. So the whole ride home was pretty quiet. She just stared out the window, and I listened to the radio."

"So that's it? Then she just took off right when you got back to her place?"

JT shook her head and pursed her lips. Her face turned red. "No. She was going to lie down, and I went in to get some of my stuff to work on at home, and that's when…" Tears streaked down her face. She blinked hard and took a few deep breaths.

Jax reached out and rubbed her shoulder. "What happened? Did you guys get in a fight?"

"No, but I almost wish we did."

Jax glanced at Izzy and then back at JT.

"It's wrecked." New tears flowed.

"JT, what's wrecked?" Izzy asked. "What are you talking about?"

"Our project. All of our work for the science fair is wrecked."

Jax felt his own blood pressure rise. "What? How?"

"We don't know how. When we went downstairs, our project was tipped upside down on the floor. It could have been her cat, I guess. He is always climbing on the counters and trying to get into stuff. I would have thought that it was too heavy for him to knock over. But if he did do it, then when it fell, the cord could have scattered the paperwork. I don't know what else it could have been. It didn't really look like it just fell off, because it was so smashed. Could someone have done it on purpose?"

Jax handed her a napkin from the dispenser on the table. "Well, I'm sure Micky's mom didn't do it, and her brother has been at their dad's house. Was anyone else there?"

She dabbed her cheeks with the tissue. "Not that I know of, and nothing else in the house seemed like it was touched, just our project."

"Were you building something that might have gotten somebody's attention? You know, something dangerous or top secret?"

The waitress returned with their drinks.

JT thanked her and waited for her to move out of hearing range. "I guess it doesn't really matter if I tell you guys now. There's no way we can repair it." She shook her head and looked down at the table. "We were trying to build a teleporter that could instantly send a small item anywhere."

Izzy's eyes widened. "Cool. Did you get it to work?"

"No, we thought we were getting close, but our test objects kept catching on fire." She smirked and let out a small laugh.

Jax was glad to see her smiling; it beat crying. "But you don't know if it was an accident or not?"

"Micky thinks it was Dylan and Carter. When we were at the Redwoods, they seemed to go out of their way to taunt us about the science fair, saying that we would never win it. And they did the same thing on skip day."

Izzy pulled off his glasses and wiped his eyes. "Yeah, but I can't really picture them sneaking into Micky's house to destroy your project. That's a lot worse than teasing."

"I know. I don't really want to accuse them without having any proof, but there's more."

Jax set his drink down. "More? Like what?"

JT sat up. Her sadness seemed to be replaced with determination. "This is gonna sound strange, but twice this week I noticed that someone had messed with my notebook with all of our diagrams and equations. On Monday, Micky and I talked to Mr. Li for a few minutes, but when we went back to our seats, my notebook was opened up to one of the diagrams. I'm sure I had closed it."

"Maybe it slid off or got bumped off your desk, and someone just picked it up for you," Izzy said.

"That's what I thought at first. But then yesterday when I opened my locker after lunch, there was my notebook, opened up to a different page of equations and sitting on top of my other books." JT held out her hands. "There's no way that I left it like that. I always close it and always carry it under my books, so it wouldn't have even been on the top."

"So whoever it was had to break in to your locker," Jax said.

"Yeah, but how could anyone do that since it only opens with my thumbprint?"

"Maybe it's coincidence and you did leave it open and just forgot. Or someone could have stolen your prints off one of your books," Jax said. "Maybe that's what happened on Monday when you were talking to Mr. Li."

Izzy nearly jumped out of his seat. "Or they could have hacked the school's security system. Who's the best hacker in school?"

"Dylan," Jax said.

Izzy pointed at him. "Exactly. He brags about being able to hack into anything."

JT looked confused. "But why would he do it? How is looking at my notebook supposed to keep us from winning the science fair?"

"Unless they are trying to steal your ideas and make one first. They could have been taking pictures of each page," Jax said.

"But that wouldn't make any sense. We could easily prove that they had stolen our ideas, and they would be in so much trouble. And if they broke into Micky's house, they could be arrested."

"I've never really trusted those guys," Izzy said. "But I doubt they would do something like that."

"Well, look at the bright side. If they did do it, then they only stole the plans to something that doesn't work," Jax said.

She laughed. "You know, at first I thought it

might have been you guys just trying to figure out what we were making, but I knew you would never break into my locker."

"You said that there's no way you can repair it, right?" Jax asked.

"No, it would take way too long, and some of the parts are too expensive."

"So what are you going to do for the science fair?" Izzy asked.

"I'm not sure. Originally, we had something else in mind that would be easy to do, but would still be pretty cool."

"We can help if you want, right, Iz?"

"Yeah."

"Thanks. When I talk to Micky, I'll see if she wants to do that." She pulled out her phone and tapped the screen a couple of times. "I'm gonna try her again." Moments later, she put the phone down. "Still no answer."

The waitress brought out their food. Jax volunteered to pray, and during the meal they discussed JT's backup plan for the science fair.

After dropping the car off at her house and catching a ride with the guys, JT sat in the back seat with her phone to her ear, her frustration mounting with each unanswered call. Micky's voicemail message came on, but JT hung up without leaving a message. She looked up and made eye contact with Jax in the rear-view mirror. "Still nothing. It's not even ringing now, just going straight to voicemail."

Jax turned onto his street. "She must have turned it off. You said she didn't take her car, though, so she couldn't have gone too far."

"Are you sure you don't want to drive around and look for her?" Izzy asked.

Jax shook his head. "Sort of like finding a needle in a haystack. You know Micky. She'll calm down in a little while and call back."

"I hope so," JT said. "But I've never seen her explode like that before."

Jax parked his mom's car in the driveway. They exited the vehicle and headed for the garage. "Since you already figured out what we built, we might as well show you how it works," Jax said. "Just don't tell anyone."

JT's face brightened. "That would be great. Maybe it will take my mind off all of this other stuff."

Jax punched in the twelve-digit security code and pressed his thumb to the scanner. After the beep, he opened the door and entered. Suddenly he stopped, and JT nearly walked right into him.

"No!"

"What's wrong?" She stepped to the side to see why Jax had yelled.

Izzy ran toward the open spot in the garage

where the time machine was normally parked. "It's gone!"

JT looked from one to the other in confusion, but then she remembered what they had made. "Very funny, guys. It looks like your cloak works pretty well. I can't even see the car."

Jax's face was red. "That's because it isn't there, JT. Somebody took it."

He looked serious, almost panicky but she wasn't going to fall for their prank. "Yeah, whatever. Stop kidding around. You said you would get me back, so I'm not buying it."

"Look, JT." Izzy walked through the open area on the floor. "Would I be able to do this if there was a car here?"

"We're not playing around," Jax said. "Somebody stole the time machine."

"But how could they get in here without the code?" Izzy asked.

Jax joined Izzy. "I don't know, but—"

"Oh no." A sickening thought raced through JT's mind. "I'm so sorry."

"What?" Jax asked.

"I wrote the code in my notebook so I wouldn't forget. If they copied my pages and lifted my prints, then they could easily get in here."

The boys looked intently at her without saying a word.

"It's all my fault."

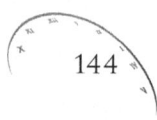

Epilogue

Bodie pulled the SUV to a stop in front of a ramshackle building on the outskirts of a small village. Looking at the faded sign next to the door, he said, "This is the place."

"Are you sure?" Rich asked, peering at the corrugated tin siding.

Bodie nodded in the direction of a man leaning up against the wall. "And that's our contact. Right next to the alley entrance."

The man walked casually to the passenger window. "Hello, strangers. Are you looking to tend some sheep?"

"Yes, we have heard there was a flock nearby, and we are shepherds."

"If I might ride with you, I can take you there."

"Thank you," Bodie said. "Please get in."

The man climbed in behind Rich and fastened his seat belt. He motioned with his hand that Bodie should start driving. After a few minutes, he spoke again. "Mister Rich and Mister Bodie, I am Hakeem, and I am so glad to see you here safe."

"Thank you, Hakeem," Bodie said. "The Lord has been gracious to us on our journeys."

"Indeed. We were very concerned for you when they made new checkpoint. But we did not know in time to warn you."

"It's not your fault," Rich said. "By God's grace

we made it safely through. We have nothing to fear with Him on our side."

"Yes, yes. You're quite right. Nothing to fear."

Thanks

The authors would like to thank all the people who helped make this series a reality. For their creative input, support, and inspiration, we thank Casey, Abigail, Kayla, Judah, Lukas, Melody, Nathanael, Roger, and Steve.

A very special thank you goes to editor extraordinaire, Reagen Reed, for turning us into better writers. This series would never have been the same without you.

We extend an extra special thank you to Melissa Mathis (a.k.a. Inkhana) for her incredible artwork. Thank you for using your talents for our Lord and Savior Jesus Christ and for your efforts to glorify Him through the use of Manga. If you like the illustrations in this series please visit Melissa's website at www.christianmanga.com and be sure to check out her books.

Finally, we thank Jesus Christ for loving us so much that He willingly died in our place and saved us from our sins. Without Him nothing is possible.

THE AUTHORS

Tim Chaffey is a husband, father, pastor, teacher, cancer survivor, author, and apologist, with a passion for reaching young people with the gospel. He earned a B.S. and M.A. in Biblical and Theological Studies, a Master of Divinity specializing in Apologetics and Theology, and a Th.M. in Church History and Theology.

Tim is the content manager for the Ark Encounter and Creation Museum. He is also the founder of Risen Ministries, which is home to his blog, podcast, and speaking ministry. He has written over a dozen books, including *The Remnant Trilogy* and *In Defense of Easter: Answering Critical Challenges to the Resurrection of Jesus*.

Joe Westbrook is a husband, father, occasional writer and blogger, aspiring theologian, and amateur woodworker. He pays the bills by working in a hospital lab, though he has ambitions to find a creative career that can be accomplished out of his home.

Joe lives in central Iowa. You can follow his exploits on Facebook by searching for Central Iowa Craftsman, Central Iowa Theologian, or Joe Westbrook Author.